"Ship's rear port has been accessed," Lizette announced. "They are entering the *Remora*."

All sound on the foredeck ceased.

"They've accessed the main gangway," was Lizette's next report. "They're heading this way."

Captain Mendez nodded and rose to her feet. "Prepare to greet our guests," she informed the room, and her officers stood after her.

Demming was glad to be on his feet again. At least it felt less passive than sitting quietly, awaiting their fate.

He could hear sounds from the gangway now, the heavy thud of feet marching toward the foredeck. Why weren't they swimming, he wondered. It was faster and easier.

As he listened, something else nagged at him. He had done plenty of marching as a cadet—it was supposed to strengthen certain leg muscles they didn't use as heavily when swimming, and to prepare them in case of a hull breach or one of the rare, risky missions to those isolated outcroppings of land above the water's surface. The beat of feet upon a deck was one he'd heard many times, and he had learned to appreciate it because it allowed him to move his own body in time and thus stay in formation with the others. But this was different. The beat was off.

He wondered what that meant.

It seemed like hours before they heard the oddly off-kilter rhythm stop just beyond the foredeck's door. There was a pause, and then the porthole irised open. Several short, ungainly figures stepped over the lower lip and entered the command cabin.

Demming gaped, and had to stop himself from sputtering up water like a child. He heard similar reactions around him, and Pyle did choke slightly, though the young midshipman managed to control himself quickly. All of them stared, however.

And with good reason.

ONCE, LONG AGO, THERE WAS ONE EARTH. It was said that many deities gazed down upon it protectively, and there was balance between them all. Then something went wrong. The balance shifted—toward darkness. Earth was shattered, her people destroyed, her remains scattered far and wide. But the gods survived the cataclysm. They scattered as well, each pursuing a fragment of their former domain. And, when they overtook those shards, the gods drew upon what power remained to them to restore their worshippers to life.

These new followers rose from dust and imperfect memory, for the gods too had been injured. Each claimed a new home, and a new life, and each thought itself—at least at first—to be the only Earth. All memory of their former world was lost, except vague memories of the gods who gave them new life. Then, one day, a single great event drew all their eyes to the stars—and beyond. And each of them felt a yearning. Something in them desired to be whole again, or at least to understand.

These are their stories.

These are The Tales of the Scattered Earth.

## AVAILABLE & UPCOMING TALES
## OF THE SCATTERED EARTH

*Second Veil*—by David Niall Wilson

"Crossed Paths"—by Aaron Rosenberg

*Guilt in Innocence*—by Keith R. A. DeCandido

*The Honor of the* Dread Remora—by Aaron Rosenberg

# THE BIRTH OF THE DREAD REMORA

## TALES OF THE *DREAD REMORA*, BOOK I

## A TALE OF THE SCATTERED EARTH

### BY AARON ROSENBERG

Mystique Press is an imprint of Crossroad Press.

Copyright © 2011 by Aaron Rosenberg
Design by Aaron Rosenberg
ISBN 978-1-948929-13-4

First edition

# CHAPTER ONE

MIDSHIPMAN NATHANIEL DEMMING GLANCED AT his pocket watch again, the luminous face easily readable through the water. T minus four to launch. *No worries, old boy,* he told himself. *After all, we're about to attempt the first launch of an untested ship with an untried crew and an uninformed captain, on a mission to an unexplored domain after an unexplained target.*

Why fret?

"T minus four to launch," Lizette Mills reported from the helm. Demming hid a smile. She was half a second off in her count, but what did that matter? And what would he possibly gain by pointing that out now? Far better to keep silent and rib her about it later, in the officers' mess. Lizette was always a fun one to rib.

"Roger that," Captain Mendez replied, sitting tall in the command chair. From his position behind her Demming could still make out the topknot of her dark blond braid beneath her cap. Not a hair out of place, as usual. "Are we secure?"

That last was directed at him, Demming realized after a heartbeat, and scanned his console, studying the readouts. "Secure, captain," he confirmed a few seconds later. His heart was thudding so loudly it was a wonder the water was rippling all around him. "All crew in their harnesses, all ports locked down."

"Good. Mister Dittmer?"

"All secure, Captain," the quartermaster replied right away, his voice as lazy as always. With any other man Demming would have assumed he had taken the time to double-check while the captain was waiting for his answer first, but with Dittmer he knew that wasn't the case. Dittmer didn't need extra time. He already knew where every scrap of material was on this ship. The man had a memory like a clamshell, latched on tight.

"T minus three," Lizette updated. Everyone on the foredeck tensed with anticipation. Behind him Demming heard someone, most likely one of the ensigns, gasp for breath—and start choking as water filled his lungs. Classic rookie mistake. A wave of quiet laughter filled the cabin. Demming could hardly blame the ensign, though. It was all he could do to keep his own mouth closed, nostrils clamped shut, gills narrowed. What he really wanted was to start gasping himself, but that would never do. He was a midshipman of the line, for current's sake! He had not only his own dignity but the dignity of the entire ship and the entire Royal Navy to maintain!

Plus the others would laugh at him just as they were all laughing at the ensign now. And that was no way to begin a mission. Especially this mission.

"T minus two."

"Throttle us up, Miss Mills," Mendez ordered. Lizette nodded, her hand going to the smooth coral inlay of the throttle and easing it down a quarter toward the console. Beneath and all around him Demming could feel the thrum as the ship's engines started to spin.

Soon. Very soon.

"T minus one."

"Ready on my mark," the captain warned. She reached for the speaking tube built into the arm of her chair, and her next words echoed faintly, as they repeated from speakers all throughout the ship. "Ladies and gentlemen, we are about to embark on our mission. I consider it an honor and a privilege to lead you into history. May the waves grant us success, and water save the queen."

"Water save the queen," Demming repeated softly, along with the other officers and, no doubt, the seamen in their compartments. And water save us, he thought. But did not say out loud.

"Mark!" Mendez hissed, and Lizette's quick fingers tapped controls, releasing the clamps that bound them to the docks and slamming the throttle down full. With a roar and a twist the ship's engines boomed to life, revving instantly to full speed, and with a mighty rushing sound the HMES *Remora* shot up from the ocean floor, her long, tapered prow pointed up at the air and at the stars beyond.

The force of their acceleration slammed Demming back in his seat, and he was grateful for the webbing that secured him there. He gripped the armrests on either side, feet planted flat on the floor, and kept his eyes squarely on the narrow windows that sliced down over the foredeck and arced along it toward its nose. For now all he could see was water, lit by the *Remora*'s powerful searchlights but shifting past too quickly to leave any real impression. This was the easy part, however. He had seen all of this before.

It was what came next that would be a shock.

In what seemed only moments but Demming knew had to be closer to an hour the water began to lighten. He could make out fish and reefs rushing by. They were nearing the surface. He felt his lungs constrict at the very thought of it.

The surface!

"Prepare for wave breach!" Lizette announced, her hand tightening on the throttle to one side and her fingers poised over the sonic pulse array to the other.

"All hands, hold fast!" Captain Mendez ordered through the speakers.

The water continued to brighten, forcing Demming to squint against the glare. He fought the instinct to turn away, or close his eyes. He had to watch this. After all, how many could say they had experienced true wave breach? And he wanted to remember all of this journey, every second, so that he could chronicle it later. For posterity.

Or for those who wondered what became of them.

With a surge of sound that set the hull ringing, the *Remora*'s prow burst upward through the waves. The light was blinding. Demming blinked, trying to clear his sight, and after a few seconds he found he could see again. It was so bright! And so empty!

His body pushed back in his chair, feeling heavy and sluggish. The *Remora* groaned around them. The noise had increased when they'd broken through, but the sense of momentum had dimmed rapidly. Now it felt as if they were barely moving, yet he could make out strange white shapes, filmy like jellyfish but puffed out like ink clouds, appearing in view and then vanishing below. So they must still be rising.

But for how long? Even now the waters exerted their hold, attempting to draw the ship back into the deeps.

"Sonic pulse on my mark!" Captain Mendez told Lizette. She didn't shout—their two chairs were less than a body-length apart—but every word was crisp and clear.

"Aye aye, captain!" Lizette tensed at the ready.

"Mark!"

The pilot's fingers jabbed down on the array, and the *Remora* shuddered as a rush of energy exploded behind her. Demming held his breath. All of this had worked in theory, and on the probe, but they had never had the chance to test it on a real ship, with a real crew.

This was the test.

Right now.

With them in it.

He waited, not sure what he was expecting. But after a second he realized that the *Remora* was still rising. If anything, her velocity had increased. It had worked!

"Again!" Mendez ordered, and Lizette complied. The ship shook again, though some of that faded as Lizette throttled down the impellers to three-quarter speed, and the *Remora* leaped skyward again, forced upward by the focused sonic burst it had just released behind.

And above—

Demming peered through the window. The sky was lighter and lighter in color as they rose, approaching pure white now, and through it he could just make out the twinkling of lights.

The stars.

They were close.

"How soon?" Mendez demanded. The question didn't seem aimed at anyone in particular, so it was her first lieutenant, Daniel Holst, who answered.

"Fifty kilometers and closing, captain," he reported. "And all systems are performing admirably."

"Thank you, Mister Holst." Demming could hear the smile

in her voice. "Miss Mills, please continue."

"Yes, captain." Lizette fired off another sonic pulse, the energy wave pushing off the waves and earth below and propelling the *Remora* further. The pressure was immense, slamming everyone into their seats, causing whines and creaks from spots along the hull and around the inner port, making it hard to breathe, hard to focus, hard to think. Demming kept his eyes trained on the stars beyond and took short, shallow breaths, letting the water filter into his gills almost of its own accord. The scientists had all agreed this pressure would let up once they breached the air. And they were so close! Almost— almost—

*Wham!*

The *Remora* lurched as if she had slammed into a strong current head-on. The ship flipped onto its side, all its momentum spent, listing and drifting with the dregs of that lost velocity. Water buffeted Demming, slapping his face and hands and chest and legs, and again he resisted the impulse to gulp for breath. Beyond the window, the glare had suddenly winked out, replaced by a darkness as deep as any abyss. There had been no lights in the cabin—none had seemed necessary—and in the sudden darkness only the telltales on various consoles could be seen. And here and there the gleam of those lights reflected in wide, terrified eyes.

And there was silence.

Demming had found the noise deafening as they'd shot through the air, but its absence was far worse. He had expected normal sounds, if slightly diminish—the roll of the waves, the rush of water through the impellers, the hum of the engines, the song of whales and chatter of dolphins and flutter of fish.

Here? Here there was nothing.

Everyone, it seemed, was holding their collective breath.

And then the sounds came all at once. But only from within the *Remora* herself.

Shouting. Whispering. Cursing. Whimpering. Even crying.

The ship generated its own wave of noise as crew and officers alike began to panic.

Demming fought down his own urge to do likewise. This would not do! This was a ship of the line! They had their honor to maintain!

He forced himself to calm down, to breathe slowly and evenly. He unclenched his hands where they had dug into the armrests. He uncurled his toes and set his feet flat against the floor once more. And he waited.

Waited for the captain to tell them what to do.

Captain Mendez was an experienced captain. Not of a ship like this, of course—no one was. But she had years of training handling other vessels, and crews this size and even larger. She was quiet and competent and very much by-the-books. He knew that, once she had taken time to collect herself, she would regain control and restore order.

So Demming waited.

The seconds seemed to stretch on. The cacophony did not diminish. If anything, it grew in volume and diversity as more of his shipmates found their voice. There was thrashing as many wrestled with their harnesses, and banging throughout the *Remora* indicated that at least some had already worked their way free, though to what end Demming could not imagine.

He was content to sit and await orders.

Until he heard the one thing he had feared the most.

It began as a whisper. Rapidly it grew into a wail, a single ululation that sound spread into words.

Words that chilled him to the very soul.

"Oh, great wave!" were the words that struck terror into his heart and blood. "Great wave, we're lost! We've been consumed by the abyss! Our souls will be devoured by the darkness!"

All other sounds on the foredeck ceased, then, as every officer turned to stare at the command chair—and their tall, blond captain, who curled up in it, sobbing and crying out in despair.

# CHAPTER TWO

*IT ISN'T SUPPOSED TO BE like this!* Demming thought desperately, gritting his teeth to keep his own cries from escaping where they had begun rising like bile in his throat. *This isn't how we were told it would happen!*

His thoughts flashed back to that time a few months before, when the Queen herself had spoken to them at the Great Assembly. Then his mind wandered back still further, to when it had all begun.

He had been in the gymnasium, he remembered, lifting weights. He took physical fitness very seriously—he hadn't as a youth, but once he'd enrolled in cadet school Demming had begun to discover its importance. He had thrown himself into the comforting routine of working out, and had quickly lost the baby fat that had stubbornly clung to him all through his teen years, his features shifting from pleasantly soft to angularly handsome. When he had been selected for officer training he had increased his daily work-outs, putting as much effort into getting into shape as he did into his studies and the leadership exercises their instructors threw at them. And he had begun to excel at all three.

Demming had been concentrating on leg lifts, arms locked

in place at his side, hands flat on the bench to support his upper body, legs straining to raise the heavy metal rings from the base. As a result, he'd barely heard the commotion, and hadn't noticed anything until he'd finished his reps and let the rings drop back down with a clatter, collapsing with a sigh against the bench's padded back.

That was when he realized everyone else in the gymnasium was clustered around the large, curved window that took up one wall.

"What's going on?" he asked, levering himself up and floating across to join the others. They were all gazing upward, craning their necks to peer out past the gym's sloping roof, and Demming looked in that direction as well, though he didn't know what he was looking for.

"There!" someone in front shouted. "I see it!"

"Where?" a dozen others replied. Then a second took up the cry: "Yes! I see it too! It's right there!"

Demming peered with the others. What were they all looking at? He saw nothing in that direction save the endless ocean, an unremarkable trawler drifting past with its bulging nets, a few fish darting about, and—

—what was that?

"What is that?" he asked softly, squinting to see more clearly. There was something there, something behind the trawler and the fish, something that seemed to be coming from up above.

Something bright.

Very bright.

As he stared, the light resolved itself. It was definitely bright, but he couldn't make out any shape, any edges. It was merely a glow. A small one, too—no bigger than his thumb from this vantage, though Demming suspected it was far larger than that. Especially because he had a feeling he was seeing that light from a great distance.

But how great?

Was it something in the upper waters?

Or could it be beyond even that?

"Amazing," someone beside him whispered, and Demming turned. It was Talbert Reeves, one of his fellow cadets.

"Tal, what's going on?" Demming asked him quietly. "What's with that light?"

His classmate turned and glanced up at him, for Tal was ironically not very tall. "Didn't you hear?" He snorted at Demming's headshake. "Let me guess, you were too busy studying—or exercising." The snort became a chuckle. "Look around you, Nate—get your head out of those books and your eyes off those weights. There's a whole world going on here!"

"Just tell me what happened," Demming asked again. He didn't mind the ribbing. He knew Reeves was just teasing him.

"Did you see the light?" Reeves nodded. "That's what's going on! There was an announcement, just a few minutes ago. You might have heard it, if you were paying any attention! The Royal Science Brigade said they'd spotted something strange, a small, bright light."

"So what?" Many of the others were still plastered by the window but Demming drifted back toward the weight equipment, and Reeves floated alongside him. "So it's a light? Big deal."

"It is a big deal," his classmate insisted. "Because it's not in the water."

"Up in the air?" That was news. They rarely went above the waves—there was nothing there but fierce winds and glaring sunlight and driving rain, and a few small, dreary clusters of rock and soil. The sunlight filtered down to them, of course, but it was a gentle, diffuse light, nothing like this tiny, glaring presence.

"Not in the air." Reeves looked like he was about to burst, his round face turning red with glee. "Beyond!"

"Beyond the air?" Demming reached out and grasped the nearest machine, halting his forward motion and leaning on the equipment while his thoughts raced on ahead. Beyond the air? That was impossible!

Scientists had been arguing about what lay beyond the air for years. The air had a definite end, they claimed, and a few airborne probes had seemed to support that theory. There was a curvature to the air, just as there was to the water, with one globe surrounding the other. And both globes had an outer limit. Beyond water and wave was air. But what lay beyond air? That was the question, and one no one had a clear answer for.

Or, rather, there were plenty of answers. But no one could prove any of them.

Some felt there was nothing, that the air was the limit of their world and beyond was emptiness. That seemed unlikely, as anything that could form such a complex system as their world—call it the Creator or the Scientific Principle or the Laws of Causality—would not have stopped with them. What force would leave a single world hanging in a void? Why not continue to create, and fill that space with other objects, even other worlds?

Others felt that past the air must be more water, so that they were a water bubble within an air bubble within a much larger ocean, one that stretched farther than they could comprehend. If that were the case, they argued, Man could traverse the air and reach the outer water and live there as well. That was a tantalizing thought, but not without risk. What if they were wrong? What would happen to those men and women who did make the journey upward and outward?

Still others felt there was something beyond the air but that it was not water. They argued that air was lighter than water, which was why it filled the space above the waves. Whatever was beyond the air, then, would have to be even lighter. They had dubbed that theoretical substance "ether," and suggested that it filled a vast space beyond the world, and possibly contained other worlds like flowers floating in a calm pool.

There were lights up above the air. That much they knew— they had seen them with airborne probes, when the sun had vanished below the horizon and allowed the smaller, fainter pinpricks to become visible. But there were as many theories about those lights and their meaning as there were about what held them, or about the meaning of life in general.

None of those theories, as far as Demming knew, allowed for the possibility of a new light.

Especially one so bright it could be seen down here in the deeps.

"What do you think it is?" Reeves asked him as Demming released the machine he'd been clutching and let himself float back toward his own weight bench.

"I have no idea," Demming admitted, sinking down onto the bench and reaching down to lift a hand weight just so he could feel its comforting bulk cold in his hand. "But I have a feeling it's going to change everything."

A week later, his guess had been proven correct. That was when the Queen's Royal Science Advisor had made an announcement.

Demming had been in a lecture at the time, but the instructor had halted her lesson so that they could all listen to the words spilling from the speaker.

"People of the world," the advisor had stated, "your attention, please! By now all of you know about the unprecedented phenomenon we observed a few short days ago. A bright, almost blinding light that lit up the night yet seemed to emanate from beyond the waves." He took a deep breath. "My colleagues and I have studied this phenomenon carefully, and with Her Majesty's kind permission we are now prepared to share some of our preliminary findings. The most important of which is this—that light did indeed come from beyond the water, beyond the air, and beyond our world."

A ripple of sound swept through the lecture hall, and the instructor waved them all to silence as the advisor's voice continued.

"That the light's origins are beyond the limits of our world we have determined without a doubt. Probes sent up into the air registered the same light, only more intense, and isolated its location in the sky. But the distance readings were incredible, almost impossible to credit. They were of such a magnitude that our finest instrumentation could not calculate them. Further, each probe rose to its maximum height in the tumultuous air, and pinpointed the light's location as best it could. But comparing their calculations, the only way to reconcile them was if the light came from beyond the air, and indeed at such a distance as to appear to be in the same fixed location from several observational points."

He paused for breath again, or for dramatic effect, and again there was a wave of murmuring. Demming did not participate—his attention was locked on the speaker, and the strange new information emanating from it.

"The light's presence, and its sudden appearance, have led us to conclude that one of the prevailing theories about what lies beyond our world must be correct." Everyone leaned forward eagerly, Demming among them. "The light's unwavering nature indicates that it did not travel through water before reaching the air above, yet its existence shows clearly that there is more than emptiness beyond. Therefore, our world must be surrounded by ether, and in that lighter-than-air substance other objects and perhaps even other worlds exist."

Now the murmur rose to a flood, as everyone turned to argue or ponder or crow to their neighbors. Demming stayed silent.

"Her Majesty has authorized us to begin further studies on this matter," the advisor stated, and Demming strained to hear him through all the noise. "We firmly believe that the light indicates other objects in the ether, and its occurrence suggests those things are no more static than our own world. Discovering the location and nature of the light would provide us with answers as to the nature of the universe in which we exist, and might well reveal other great truths such as how our own world was created. In the days and weeks to come, we will be consulting with other scientists and scholars as how best to proceed, and we will keep Her Majesty and the public advised as we make new discoveries. Thank you."

"Can you believe it?" One of the other students asked Demming as the announcement ended and the speakers' sound faded to a faint crackle of static before switching off entirely. "Ether! Amazing!"

"Amazing," Demming agreed. But he was not really listening. His mind was awhirl. Ether, indeed! That was not the important part, however. No, what he had latched onto was the advisor's closing remarks. "Discovering the location and nature of the light," he had said. They would send probes first, of course. But probes could only be trusted so far, especially in such unfamiliar territory. To really discover the truth, there was only one answer:

A ship.

Somehow, they would have to send a ship out into the ether.

Where no one had ever gone before.

Demming leaned back, his fingers absently knitting themselves together atop his books. A grin began to stretch its way across his face.

*I will be on that ship,* he vowed.

# CHAPTER THREE

AND HERE I AM, DEMMING reminded himself grimly, fingers tightening on his armrests. *Just like I said.*

*Only now it looks like I may die here, only moments after we've breached the air.*

The thought made him growl softly, and an answer erupted in his head, thrumming simultaneously through his blood:

*No.*

*No, I don't think so.*

*I will not die like this,* he declared silently. *Not strapped into my chair like an old man unable to navigate his way to the head, and not on the thinnest edge of the greatest adventure mankind has ever conceived. That is simply unacceptable.*

He closed his eyes for a second, filtering out the moans and whimpers that had begun to spring back up, and the continuing sound of Mendez's wails. Blocking it all out. He took several slow, deep breaths, forcing his own heart to calm.

Then he snapped his eyes back open.

First things first.

Swiveling his head about, Demming took in as much of the cabin as he could. The *Remora* had been built partially along standard scoutship lines, and he'd been well familiar with

those from his training even before the hours of drilling here.
He knew the cabin's shape and dimensions, knew its layout,
knew where each station was placed. Ahead of him were
Lizette and the captain, and just behind the captain's chair were
the two lieutenant's posts, one to either side. Holst was to the
right, as befitted his rank as first lieutenant, and Gist Jacobsen,
second lieutenant, was on the left. Then his own station and
the quartermaster's. Behind them were the two ensigns, Pyle
and Craddick. Jeremy Pasic, the ship's doctor, had a solitary
post by the door, where he could get out and down the hall in
a hurry if there was a problem elsewhere. And that was it. The
*Remora*'s other officers were in their own places: Amelia Scott,
chief engineer, was down in the engine room where she could
deal with any trouble immediately, while Howell Kesselman,
the boatswain, was in the general crew compartment to make
sure the regular sailors kept calm. On a normal scout ship the
ship's gunner would be in the weapons room, near the firing
controls, but this was an exploratory mission into what was
thought to be empty ether, so Molly Cuny was with the general
crew instead. So was Quentin Watkins, unless he had insisted
on staying in the ship's galley during launch—a foolish notion,
but Quentin took his duties as cook very seriously.

So. Nine of them here on the foredeck. Demming could see
Lizette, who was standing stock-still, one hand clutching the
throttle as if it were a lifeline, the other placed palm-flat atop the
sonic pulse controls. Mendez was still curled up and sobbing.
Holst—Demming studied him, eyes narrowing to piece the
gloom and the distance and the water, then widening as they
registered what they were seeing. Holst lolled in his harness,
unconscious. Or worse.

Demming craned his neck, trying to see around the chair

directly in front of him. What about Jacobsen? After a second he saw movement, just wriggling but enough to confirm that the second lieutenant was at least awake. Good enough for now.

Dittmer was not moving, however. The distance across the deck was great enough that Demming could not make out if the quartermaster was breathing or not. His head was back, at least, rather than loose to one side like Holst's. That was a good sign, though he'd have to get closer to make sure.

That accounted for the four in front of him, and the one alongside. There was no way he could see behind him, not while he was still strapped in.

Which answered the question of what to do next.

Demming let his fingers stroke down the harness's webbing until they slid from smooth rubber to cool metal. There! It was harder to work the complicated, double-safety clasp without light, but they'd trained for situations like this and his fingers knew what to do. After a few seconds of struggle they found the right combination of pressure points and the harness released with an audible click. Demming swallowed a sigh of relief as he shrugged free of the webbing. Too much left to do to celebrate just yet.

Still, it felt almost sinfully good to brace his feet, tense his legs, and shove off, floating upward out of his seat and letting the warm water buoy him. Effortlessly he turned to study the trio behind him. Pyle's eyes were wide and staring, reflecting the dim light of the consoles, while Craddick's seemed to be squeezed shut. No help there.

But Pasic—Pasic sat upright in his seat, his head shifting slightly to follow Demming's movement, but the rest of him still. Demming drifted closer, a slight kick carrying him most of the distance, and the ship's doctor smiled as he approached.

"Mister Demming," Pasic said softly as Demming reached him and grabbed the handhold built into the doorframe to steady himself. "Good of you to check on me."

"Just doing my job, doctor," Demming replied, the light banter helping to calm him further. It was true, too, as far as that went—as midshipman, part of Demming's job was to help the captain and her lieutenants make sure the officers and crew were all safe. Right now he was simply doing that without their orders. "How are you feeling, sir?" Technically Pasic outranked him, though a ship's doctor wasn't in the command structure.

"Fine, thank you," Pasic answered. Demming could see his long, handsome features slacken slightly as the doctor seemed to consider the question fully. "Heartbeat is racing, blood is rushing, slight lightheadedness—I'd say we were experiencing significantly decreased pressure."

Demming nodded. He'd noticed, somewhere in the back of his brain, that he'd lifted into the water with very little effort, and had floated up farther than he'd expected—far enough that he'd had to duck his head to keep from grazing the ceiling. "We knew that would likely be the case," he pointed out. "The ether is supposed to be lighter than air, after all. At least the hull pressurization seems to have held." If it hadn't, the sudden decrease in pressure would have given them all bends, ruptures, and worse.

"Indeed." Pasic's face creased in a tight smile. "I assume you did not leave your post to discuss my health, or the ship's status, however?"

"No, sir." Demming glanced behind him, toward the command chair. "Can you do anything for her, sir?"

The doctor frowned, then nodded. "Yes, I believe so." He unlatched his own harness—with only a little more fumbling than Demming, Demming was pleased to see—and reached beneath his chair for the emergency medical kit stowed there. Then he rose into the water and drifted up alongside Demming. "I can give her something to calm her down, at least," he explained softly, his words barely carrying through the water. "What will you do?"

Demming grinned at him. "Try to snap everyone out of this," he answered.

In truth, he had no plan beyond that. That was typical for him, however. "Doesn't plan well in advance," his evaluations had reported, and he couldn't really argue that. He tended to act first and think about the consequences later.

At least his instructors had been honest enough to add, "Has excellent instincts, however, and typically does the right thing, even if sometimes in an unusual way."

That's what he was counting on now. Right, even if it was unusual.

As Pasic slid past him, Demming turned to the two ensigns. "Snap out of it, lads!" he told them sharply. Pyle jerked upright, hand leaping up into a salute. Craddick just hunched in further and shook his head. "Mister Craddick!" Demming let a little more iron seep into his voice. "Enough lollygagging! Hop to it, man!"

That did the trick. Craddick's eyes popped open, and he straightened and saluted, some color returning to his face as he flushed slightly. "Yes, sir! Orders, sir?"

"The two of you get to the crew quarters and locate Mister Kesselman," Demming instructed. "Make sure he has everything under control down there."

"Aye aye, sir!" Craddick wrenched at his harness, trying to tear it off first before calming down and remembering how to work the clasp. Pyle, who had stayed calmer, was already out of his chair and turning toward the door by the time Craddick got loose.

As the door slid open, however, Pyle glanced back at Demming. "Will we—will we be okay, sir?" the young ensign asked. The shakiness in his voice said he was close to tears.

"We'll be fine, Mister Pyle," Demming assured him with as much confidence as he  could muster. "Now get along to the bo'sun."

"Aye, sir." The two ensigns disappeared down the gangway, and the door slid shut again behind them.

That was two more taken care of, Demming congratulated himself after they had gone. If Kesselman needed help, they would lend a hand and push back their own panic by concentrating on what had to be done. If not, they would see that the crew were maintaining their calm and would be reassured by it. Either way, the ensigns would be better for their little trip. Assuming, of course, that they didn't find mass chaos and a pile of corpses in the crew quarters, but Demming pushed that grisly thought away as quickly as it appeared. No sense borrowing trouble.

Pasic had reached the captain by this point, and was bending over her, murmuring something even as his hands drew two small objects from the medical kit. A sedative and a syringe, no doubt. Demming knew he could leave the doctor handle that situation, so he turned his own attention toward the quartermaster. A short flip-kick carried him to Dittmer's seat, and he was relieved to see the man's chest rising and falling steadily. Just knocked out, then. Good.

Next on the list was Daniel Holst. The news there was less positive, however. As Demming swam across to the first lieutenant's chair, he saw that Holst's position had not changed. He still hung in his harness, his head to one side, his long red hair bobbing in the gentle current Demming's approach created. Close up, he saw that Holst's eyes were open and staring, his tongue partially out of his mouth and turning blue. The man was clearly dead.

Damn.

Demming reached out, cursing his hands as they shook, and closed Holst's eyes. He'd liked the first lieutenant. Everybody had. Holst was one of those officers who was good at what he did but not arrogant about it, and who always had time for a smile and a nod and a word of encouragement. He'd be sorely missed.

Glancing up, Demming saw that Pasic was watching him. He shook his head. Even with almost no light he could see the tall doctor's shoulders slump.

Light. That should be his next priority. Everything looked less terrifying with light.

Demming turned back toward the chair behind Holst's—he just couldn't bring himself to use the dead man's console. Instead he borrowed Dittmer's, and activated the quartermaster's speaking tube.

"Miss Scutt? Miss Scutt, this is Mister Demming, on the foredeck. Do you read me?" He paused for a second. "Amelia? Are you there?"

There was nothing but silence, and he felt his heart lurch. Not Amelia! Then her voice crackled through the console's tiny speaker.

"Nate? Oh, thank the wave! What happened? We breached and then everything went crazy. My instruments are going nuts, the readings don't make any sense, the impellers cut out, and—what are you doing hailing me from the quartermaster's station?"

"Dittmer's unconscious," he explained quickly. "So is the captain, I think." He took a quick breath. "Holst is dead."

"Dead? No! How?"

"Snapped his neck—I think that sudden lurch during the breach did it."

"Oh, that's terrible!" She started sobbing.

"Amelia, we need the lights," Demming told her softly. "I don't know how the rest of the crew's holding up, but sitting here in the dark isn't helping anyone. Can you get us up and running again?"

"If by running you mean moving under full power, not a chance," she answered, audibly swallowing tears as she concentrated on his questions. "Maybe once I've had a chance to study everything, figure out what happened, but not right now." She paused and took what sounded like several deep breaths. "But lights? That I can do. I've just got to reroute power from the auxiliary systems. Give me a minute."

"Take whatever you need," Demming told her. He started to turn away from the console, then stopped. "I'm glad you're okay."

"Thanks. I'm glad you are, too." There'd been a smile in those words, he was sure of it. Then she'd signed off.

Looking up from Dittmer's station, Demming glanced around and saw that Pasic was speaking with Lizette, sleek dark hair lowered over shimmering black waterfall. That only left Jacobsen, so Demming kicked off across the cabin and angled toward the second lieutenant's chair. Jacobsen was thrashing about, and his frenzy increased as he caught sight of Demming.

"Get me out of here!" he demanded, writhing in his harness.

But even someone as powerfully built as the athletic second lieutenant wasn't going to able to force those strands apart. His voice, normally low and self-assured, sounded high and rapid, just shy of panic.

"Hang on," Demming assured him, keeping his own tone calm and his voice low. He leaned in to study the situation, and almost got decked for his troubles as Jacobsen's fist just missed grazing his cheek. "Hey, now! Just settle down! I'll have you out of this in a jiffy, but only if you can hold still long enough for me to help!"

The second lieutenant stilled slightly. "Sorry," he offered, and managed a quick laugh that threatened to become giggling. "I'm just—I can't seem to get loose." His usual good looks were mussed and harried, his dark skin oddly pale, his blue eyes widely dilated.

"I understand." Demming still couldn't see much, so he grasped Jacobsen's harness and let his fingers explore the webbing. "Ah." Somehow in his thrashing the second lieutenant had twisted a bit of the harness around and over the clasp, knotting it into the webbing and making it impossible to reach or open. Demming tried to untangle the mess, but it was too gnarled and he couldn't see if he was helping matters or making them worse. Finally he sighed and leaned back.

"You've got a piece of your harness twisted," he explained. "I can't undo it. I'll need to cut you free." He reached for his boot and drew his diving knife.

"What?" Jacobsen went rigid at the statement, and his eyes almost burst from his head when he saw the slim blade glittering in the dim light. "Are you crazy? You're going to cut me out? And where'd you get that? That's not regulation!"

Which was true—the diving knife wasn't official Royal

Navy issue. But officers were allowed personal items, including small blades and sidearms. And Demming's grandfather had presented him with the knife when he'd graduated from school and become a cadet. "Every sailor needs a good knife," Granddad Jonas had explained. "I had this one from my own father, and it's always served me well. It'll do the same for you."

Demming had rarely had to use it. But he was glad he had it now.

"Trust me," he assured Jacobsen, grasping the harness in one hand just above the troublesome snarl and bringing the knife closer with the other. "This will only take a second." The knife's sharp edge made short work of even the reinforced webbing, and with a faint twang that section parted, exposing the clasp. Demming slid the blade back into his boot sheath and hit the harness release. "There you are."

"Move!" Jacobsen shoved him aside and launched out of his chair, cursing softly a second later as he crashed headlong into the ceiling and rebounded.

"Pressure's a bit low," Demming warned belatedly. "Watch your head." He wasn't overly fond of the second lieutenant, who'd always been a bit arrogant, and the current performance wasn't doing anything to endear the man to him further.

"Got it." To his credit, Jacobsen chuckled as he floated back down a bit. "Thanks." He extended a hand. "And thanks for getting me loose. Sorry I was terse with you. Just—" A hand waved at the rest of the cabin took in their situation.

"Of course." Demming shook his hand, and mentally accepted the apology. No reason not to.

Just then, the lights came on.

"Ah, much better!" Pasic said, gliding over to them with Lizette in tow, his tall, angular frame a sharp contrast to her short, curvy one. She still seemed a little dazed, but at least she was conscious and glancing about. "Everything all right with you two?"

"Fine, sir," Demming answered. He risked a glance toward the command chair. "How's the captain?"

"Sleeping it off. She should be fine." Pasic looked across to the quartermaster. "And Mister Dittmer?"

"Breathing normally, sir. I think he got knocked out during the breach."

"Most likely. I'd better check on him." Pasic shook his head. "Damn shame about Holst, though."

"Holst? What—" Jacobsen's voice trailed off as he looked over and saw the state of his former superior officer. "Ah." The sight of the dead man seemed to sap what little energy he'd regained from his recent freedom.

Demming allowed the man a moment. Then he spoke quietly. "Any orders, sir?"

"What?" The look Jacobsen turned his way was equal parts frustration, surprise, and fear.

"You are now acting first lieutenant, sir," Demming pointed out. "And with the captain incapacitated, you're in charge. What are your orders?"

Jacobsen studied him, eyes narrowing as if seeking the joke. Then, realizing there was none, his brow unfurrowed and he nodded. "Yes, of course. Uh—"

"I sent Pyle and Craddick to check in with Mister Kesselman, sir," Demming offered. "And I've already spoken with Miss Scutt, who is unharmed. She rerouted auxiliaries to bring up the lights. Shall I coordinate with Mister Kesselman to make sure everyone else is unharmed and then check in with her to see what can be done about getting us underway once more?"

The acting first lieutenant nodded. "Yes, very good, Mister Demming. See to it."

"At once, sir." Demming saluted and launched himself toward the door. Behind him he could hear Jacobsen speaking with Lizette, telling her to determine their current location as best she could and then stand ready for further orders.

He waited until he was safely in the gangway, with the foredock port closed firmly behind him, before rolling his eyes and shaking his head.

# CHAPTER FOUR

As promised, Demming's first stop was the crew quarters. He let his mind wander, however, as he swam quickly down the main gangway, which seemed wide and spacious now with no one else about. He still remembered the first time he'd entered these sleek, handhold-studded passages.

"It's called the *Remora*," the instructor had explained to him and the other four candidates clustered behind her. "On account of the forward hatch design." Demming nodded. He'd studied the ship's plans, of course, and knew the engineers had chosen to place the main hatch near the ship's prow, just above the main crew quarters, to facilitate an easy exodus if one should prove necessary. A second, smaller hatch was set in the rear over engineering, and a third was on the ship's belly. They weren't taking any chances about the crew getting caught inside if there was a problem.

The crew. He'd smiled at that word. He'd been right, of course. The queen had intended from the first to send an exploratory team out beyond the air to investigate the light and its source. And she had, of course, turned to the Royal Navy to fulfill that goal. After all, who was better suited than the sailors and scouts and commanders already at sea?

At the same time, the Royal Navy's admirals had realized that many of their finest sailors and officers were unsuited for this mission. They were too old, too hidebound, too set in their ways. Whatever ship the royal engineers designed would need new systems and new structures to manage the flight beyond the air, and its crew would need to be able to think in new ways. They were better off taking some of their more promising trainees and letting them learn the new ship without any preconceptions.

Trainees like Demming.

He had been waiting outside Commander Robbins' office first thing the morning after the queen's proclamation. The chief instructor had raised one bushy eyebrow when he'd spotted Demming standing there, but the slight smile that formed under his equally bushy mustache suggested he hadn't really been all that surprised.

"Cadet Demming," he'd said, opening the door and ushering Demming inside. "What can I do for you?"

"The new ship, sir," Demming had replied at once. "The one that will be breaching the air. I want to be on it."

"Do you, now?" Robbins had stroked his sideburns. "And what makes you so sure there will even be one, much less that we'll be considering untrained whelps like yourself for crew?"

Demming had been undeterred by the comment. He liked Robbins. The man was a veteran seaman and an excellent instructor, very direct and very clear on his expectations, ready to judge cadets on their own merits, tough but fair.

He'd explained his reasoning, and after he'd finished the commander had nodded.

"Well reasoned," Robbins admitted. "And accurate, as far as I know. No direct word has come down yet, you understand, but a few of us have guessed the same as you, including the intention to use recruits and cadets and junior officers where possible." He'd eyed Demming again. "And what, you're hoping to captain this new vessel, are you?"

That had been a test, and Demming had kept the smile from his face when he answered. "No, sir! The captain will need to have proven experience at running a ship. I just want to be onboard, sir. Preferably as an officer, but I'll sign on as crew if that's what it takes."

"Give up your officer status for a berth, eh?" Robbins hadn't bothered to hide his own smile, or the chuckle that followed it. "Well, now! That's a noble sacrifice indeed!" He'd clapped a hand on Demming's shoulder. "No promises, lad. But when they ask for names, yours'll be on the list, never fear. And not as a common sailor, either."

"Thank you, sir!" Demming had saluted and let himself be steered back to the door and out of it. He'd swum away, sure he'd at least have a chance to prove why he should be including in this historic mission. He couldn't ask for much more.

A week later, he'd been summoned to Robbins' office and told that he would be part of an elite training class. They hadn't been given any more details, but Demming had grinned ear-to-ear as he floated away. He knew what it had to mean. He was in!

Their training had begun a week later. There were thirty officer candidates in all, and Demming had guessed that only as many as half would be chosen in the end. He heard that there were roughly a hundred crew trainees, but their requirements were less severe and so the cutoffs would be more relaxed. After all, good crew were expected to follow orders. Good officers had to know how to give orders, and what orders to give.

It had been a month before they were even shown the first plans for the ship. During that time they'd drilled on what to expect from the ether, and what controls might be in place on the ship, but the rest of the time had simply been standard training courses. The engineers had still been working on the ship's design, and until that was finished the officer candidates and crew trainees couldn't practice further.

When the ship designs had first arrived, Demming and the others had pored over them carefully. It was based on a standard manta-class scout ship, he saw at once, with the typical long, sleek body, narrow-nosed prow, and raised central foredeck. Twin impellers ran down the sides, providing propulsion, but there had been questions from the start as to whether that would be enough. The tubes worked beautifully under the waves, of course, where their rotors drew water in and then spun it about to dramatically increase velocity before shoving it out the tube's rear. The result was a fast, quiet, efficient means of travel, literally drawing from the water and then hurling it back out to push the ship forward. But impellers were less effective in the air, where the substance was so much thinner and could not generate as much thrust. If the ether was thinner still, how would they generate enough pressure to create any sort of usable velocity?

The engineers had apparently found a way. There were multiple rotors within the impellers, and an intriguing array of filters designed to pull in as much volume as practicable and then churn it to the highest degree possible. The result should be a significant increase in pressure and momentum even in normal water, and a decent speed from lighter materials like air and ether.

He'd also noticed the sonic pulse array set across the

ship's stern. The Royal Navy used sonic lances for attack, and occasionally wider sonic pulses for defense and for a last-ditch weapon or to clear away obstacles. A strong, focused pulse could shatter stone and pound coral to dust. It didn't take long for Demming to realize that, directed at a solid surface, that same pulse could provide additional momentum. It would get them through the air, almost certainly, where the pulse could be directed at the rocks that comprised land above the waves. Would it help enough in the ether? No one was certain.

While the ship was being built Demming and the others had sat lectures from various engineers and scientists, all about how the ship worked and how to handle it and what to do in a crisis. One of the other candidates had quickly demonstrated a grasp for the new technology that surpassed even some of the instructors, and Demming had pegged her at once as the expedition's chief engineer. They hadn't met before—she was a year ahead of him, and had already been made ensign on one of the newer whale-class cruisers—but Demming was impressed by what he saw. And not just her engineering skills. Tall and slender, with pale skin, long, handsome features, and a long dark braid, he couldn't understand why most of his fellow cadets failed to see just how attractive Amelia Scutt was. Not that he minded the lack of competition. Their studies had provided more than enough of that, unfortunately, and though he had made a few attempts to chat her up, Demming was unable to form more than a working friendship with the quiet, serious young woman.

As their training became more grueling, a few of the candidates had dropped out or been weeded out. Some were too old for such strenuous exercises, while others proved unable to grasp the distinctions between this ship and the others they had sailed, and thus unable to handle the different methods required here. As their numbers thinned, Demming had amused himself by assigning roles and thus measuring his own chances and potential positions in return. Amelia was engineer, that was obvious. For captain he figured either Hardesty Mendez or Reed Dittmer—both had command experience but minds agile enough to adjust to the new systems here, and both were eager to be involved. Mendez had more years of leadership, while Dittmer had the more organized mind, so she would most likely get the nod as captain while he would become first lieutenant or perhaps quartermaster. Daniel Holst would have been his first choice for captain if the short, cheerful fellow had had more experience—instead Demming figured him for first or second lieutenant. Gist Jacobsen, Howell Kesselman, Marcus Andrews, and Paula Fox were all serious contenders, and Demming knew any or all of them could serve ably as first or second lieutenant, quartermaster, boatswain, and midshipman, not to mention ensign, the most junior officer rank available. Those were the same posts he was eligible for, as well—he didn't have the talent for ship's cook, or the aim for gunner, and the the ship's doctor would be selected from the Royal Medical Academy, most likely someone who had trained as a naval cadet as well. A few other candidates, like Benson Pyle and Earl Craddick, lacked the drive and skill to win the higher ranks but would stand in admirably as ensigns. That meant it would be a fight to get assigned to the ship, even as an ensign.

But it was a fight Demming was determined to win.

He'd worked hard to master each element of their training, and had impressed his instructors with his dedication, his focus, and his energy. They'd been less pleased with Demming's tendency to bend rules from time to time, though as with his earlier teachers they'd at least recognized that he only did that when following the rules perfectly jeopardized the success of the mission or the safety of the crew. "You're willing to throw out the rulebook when necessary," one of the trainers had told him during a periodic evaluation, "and that can be a useful trait. Provided it's only when necessary, and only as much as necessary. Abiding by regulations when they're counter-productive is dangerous, but so is surrendering discipline and abandoning tradition."

Demming had nodded. He'd been warned about such things before. And he agreed. The Royal Navy was a fine and honorable establishment, with a long and proud history—one he was happy to be part of. He had no intention of ditching that. But he knew there were situations where the rules simply didn't apply. Then you had to be willing to take a chance and do what felt right, rather than what tradition and orders might dictate.

Competition had thinned slightly by the time the *Remora* had been finished enough for them to tour it. Paula had torn a ligament in her knee while running an obstacle course, and the injury would take at least a month to heal and several more before she was at full strength. She was out of the running. Marcus Andrews was having some problems with the acclimation exercises, the ones designed to simulate what they could expect while traveling the ether. Demming suspected his classmate suffered from mild agoraphobia, which wasn't much of a problem under the waves but could be deadly in open air or empty ether. If he couldn't control that fear, Marcus would never pass the final exams. Demming felt his place onboard was all but assured—even if he lost out on the higher positions, he could best Pyle and Craddick and the others for one of the two ensign posts. Still, he warned himself not to get cocky.

Besides, he didn't want to settle for ensign. He was gunning for second lieutenant.

They'd roamed the *Remora* in groups of five, admiring her smooth walls and gleaming grid floors and patterned, pockmarked ceilings. As with any ship of the line, her lighting came from bioluminescent plants that grew along the ceiling above the gratings—the plants only needed water and a steady diet of minute particles, like the dead skin cells that drifted loose from sailors every day, in order to maintain a steady glow. When given a minor electrical jolt, however, they would close up and dim their lights, fearing attack. A soothing subvocal tone would cause them to relax and glow once more, and a second, higher tone impelled them to brighten, seeking additional sustenance. It was a clean, efficient system, and the scientists saw no reason it would not work just as well while traveling the ether, especially since the *Remora* herself contained everything necessary.

The standard techniques for hull pressurization were used as well, though there was an additional measure involved— as with some of the deep-sea exploration vessels, the *Remora* would have a mild electrical current flowing through her outer hull to increase her ability to withstand pressure changes, and a constant sonic vibration emanating from the hull to lessen the impact of any differences without.

Demming had half-expected the *Remora* to be built without weapons, which he felt would be a mistake. Not that there would necessarily be anything out there to threaten them, but it was better to be sure. After all, the first explorers had assumed the abysses would be empty as well—right up until a giant squid or an armored fish had devoured them. He was pleased to see the engineers had felt the same he did, and had mounted sonic lances and net-throwers and even a few old-fashioned harpoons about the *Remora*'s edges.

He liked the ship a great deal. It felt enough like the standard ships of the line to feel familiar, but distinct enough to be even more exciting. And it seemed sleek, and fast, and capable. Just what they needed.

Just where he wanted to be.

Marcus had managed to control his fears right up to the final exam, which had involved the candidates taking the *Remora* into the deeps and handling her during a mock-crisis deep in abyss. Then he had cracked. Demming had felt a pang of sympathy when he'd watched the ship dock again and had seen the instructor leading the quivering, cringing, shock-eyed candidate toward the medical offices. At the same time, he'd felt a sharp relief. Now there were only four other candidates he felt were competent enough to attain the mid-level officer ranks. And there were five positions available.

When final postings had been made, Demming had been disappointed to learn that Jacobsen had beaten him out for second lieutenant. Mendez was captain, as expected, and with Dittmer as quartermaster Holst had of course been selected for first lieutenant. Amelia had been made engineer, just as he'd predicted, and Kesselman had been appointed bo'sun. He'd met both Lizette Mills, who would be pilot, and Molly Cuny, the new gunner, and approved both choices. Quentin Watkins had been a shoe-in for cook once they'd all tasted his stew. And they'd met the medical candidates a few times, during exercises—Jeremy Pasic was one of two who'd impressed Demming, so his appointment came as no surprise either.

But all of that was secondary to the one name he'd been

watching for most closely. The only one that really mattered to him. Demming had studied the postings, and kept his face calm even as his blood had raced and his hands had clenched. There.

Nathaniel Demming. Midshipman.

He'd done it. He was going to sail the *Remora*!

"Lucky, lucky me," Demming muttered to himself as he floated down the gangway toward the ship's prow and her crew quarters. "A life of adventure, excitement, and honor."

He wasn't really objecting, however. Yes, the launch had ended unexpectedly, and they had no idea the condition of the ship or of their mission. Yes, one officer was dead and two more incapacitated. But still, they had reached the ether! They had gone beyond any previous ship, any other vessel, anything aside from the recent probes that had blazed this trail. They were pioneers!

And Demming was sure they would overcome whatever obstacles had presented. Jacobsen had been calm when he'd left the foredeck, and assuming control for now. The captain would recover from whatever Doctor Pasic had given her, and from her own fear, and resume command once more. He would make sure Kesselman had the crew under control, then speak with Amelia to find out what could be done about the ship. Once they were making headway once more, everyone would calm down. Everything would be under control.

Which did nothing to wash away the sudden chill he felt, sailing down the long gangway all on his own, with only the faint glow of the plants for company.

# CHAPTER FIVE

"MISTER KESSELMAN!" DEMMING TOGGLED THE speaker switch on the door panel. The crew quarters' port had refused to budge at his touch, and the indicator lights were red. Locked down tight. There was no sign of Pyle and Craddick, however, so he had to assume they'd made it past the door without difficulty. He hoped things were still calm on the other side.

"Mister Kesselman, it's Midshipman Demming," he tried again. "Please respond."

There was no answer for several beats. Then the indicator blinked and turned green. It had just settled into that shade when Demming heard a faint hiss and the portal irised open.

"Mister Demming." Howell Kesselman filled the opening, his solid form at least as imposing as the metal panels had been. There may have been a faint twinkle in his dark eyes, but it was difficult to tell in the shadow of the doorframe, and his rugged features were set in their usual stoic demeanor. "Good of you to visit."

"I was sent to make sure everything was all right with the crew," Demming explained, resisting the urge to glance over the bo'sun's shoulder. That would have suggested he didn't trust Kesselman to keep matters under control, which would have been rude.

Besides, he didn't hear any fighting or screaming back there.

"You could have simply radioed," Kesselman pointed out. Again Demming was unsure if the other man was teasing him. He'd never been able to get a decent read on the bo'sun. It could be that Kesselman had no sense of humor. Or it could just be that he deliberately made such potentially wry statements to keep people guessing. Though that would suggest far more imagination than he'd demonstrated thus far.

"I prefer the personal touch," Demming answered, grinning. "And I wanted to stretch my legs a little."

"Can't say I blame you for that. Far more cramped on the foredeck." Kesselman turned and slid back a step, allowing him to enter. "Well, as you can see, matters here are under control."

And Demming did see that. The first thing he saw when he entered was Pyle and Craddick, engaged in a dice game with a few of the crewmembers. The two ensigns glanced up guiltily, but relaxed when he nodded at them. He'd sent them down here to check on things, and that had been the extent of their orders. As far as he was concerned, they'd done their duty and were at liberty until Jacobsen or the captain needed them again.

There were other games being held in corners or at tables here, for the crew quarters launch station was also the crew's mess hall—launch seats with safety harnesses lined the walls, but the center of the large chamber was occupied by tables and benches, all safely bolted to the floor. A few men and women were reading, others were chatting, one or two were doing warm-up exercises. Everything was perfectly calm.

"We had a touch of panic after that bump," the bo'sun admitted, drifting over beside Demming, "and when the lights went out. But I got that sorted quickly enough, and once the

lights came back up everyone relaxed. Now we're just waiting."
He studied Demming. "What word from the foredeck?"

"The captain's temporarily incapacitated," Demming
replied, keeping his voice low enough that only Kesselman
would hear him. No sense worrying the crew or getting them
worked up again. "Holst is dead—the bump snapped his neck.
Jacobsen's in charge until the captain recovers. Everyone else is
fine."

"And the ship?"

"I'm on my way to engineering now," Demming assured
him. "No panic lights on the consoles, and the hull seems
intact—I suspect we'd have known right away if that weren't
the case. I'm hoping Miss Scutt can tell me more about what
happened and why, and what we need to do to get underway
again."

"Well, we're ready," the bo'sun told him, gesturing at the
men and women under his command. "And a little organized
activity would not go amiss."

"Understood." Demming paused to consider. "I'm sure a few
things got tossed about during that lurch, despite precautions.
Might not be a bad idea to comb the ship, mark any damage,
and stow any loose items again."

A flash of relief crossed Kesselman's face. "I'll get people
on it at once." This was why he made a good bo'sun but would
probably never rise about that rank, Demming thought as he
took his leave and turned back toward the portal. Kesselman
was a decent bloke, solid and reliable, and excellent at following
orders. He related well to others, which was why he did well as
a bo'sun, where his job was overseeing the crew. But he lacked
imagination or initiative. He could follow orders but couldn't
conceive new ones except in the most limited sense. There was

certainly a place for that onboard a ship, but it wasn't in the upper command ranks.

"Oy, Demming!" The call brought him up short, and he was already smiling as he swiveled to face the wiry little man floating toward him. Quentin Watkins wasn't all that big on protocol. But then, as the ship's cook he didn't have to be.

"Mister Watkins. What can I do for you?" Demming liked Quentin. Though he looked thoroughly disreputable, with his scraggly hair, narrow features, and crooked smiles, Quentin was one of the nicest people Demming had ever met. He also took his work, and his food, very seriously. Which was why his answer didn't surprise Demming in the least.

"Can we get the galley open? A good hot meal'd help settle nerves as well as stomachs."

Demming pondered that. "I'm on my way to engineering, to see what's what," he answered after a second. "Best not to fire up the stoves until we're sure there aren't any problems—I'd hate to learn that we'd lost half our induction coils and needed to ration after you'd put together a feast."

"Aye, fair enough." Quentin scratched at his chin, where a few unruly whiskers had already sprung up. "Let me check it over though, at least. Make sure there's no damage, put things right if they've tumbled."

"Fair enough. And you can prepare something cold, if you like." The cook's quick, slightly guilty grin said he'd been planning that anyway, and Demming laughed. Yes, he liked Quentin.

Since he was here, Demming decided he'd better check on the other specialist in the crew quarters. He found her at the end of the farthest table, a book open before her, long dark curls shielding her dusky face from view. For such a pretty girl Molly

Cuny made a surprising effort to escape notice.

"Miss Cuny." Out of courtesy Demming slipped onto the bench opposite her, rather than looming in the water above her or beside her. "Everything all right?"

"Fine." The one word answer was a mere whisper, and she didn't glance up from the page.

"Good, good. It seems likely that bump was merely the breach, but given the tumult it might be wise to check the weapons, make sure everything's ship-shape."

She closed the book at once and drifted up from her seat without a word.

"Perhaps you should take someone with you," Demming suggested, floating up beside her. But not too close. A few of the other cadets had learned to their chagrin that the tiny, pretty little girl with the big eyes and the dark curls liked her space. And was a crack shot with anything that could be fired or thrown. He eyed the book in her hand warily.

"No." That and a headshake were the only answer he was likely to get. Demming knew he could order Pyle or Craddick to accompany her, and she'd obey. But it really wasn't necessary. There wasn't any threat right now, and even if there was another person in the weapons room would only get in her way. With a nod that she probably didn't even see Demming let her swim off. He caught Quentin's headshake and smile and knew the cook had followed that brief interaction. Demming swallowed a laugh. Quentin had been one of the first to learn to respect Molly Cuny's personal space.

Demming stopped by Pyle and Craddick to let the two ensigns know that they could remain here until further orders, then made his way toward the door. Molly Cuny had already vanished through it, and Kesselman was floating beside it, one beefy hand casually latched onto a handhold as he waited as if to escort Demming out. Which might be the case—this was Kesselman's domain, and he had a right to feel slightly protective when another officer invaded it.

"I'll relay word once I know anything else," Demming told the bo'sun as he exited, "or Jacobsen will."

"Fine." Kesselman nodded, already hitting the switch to cycle the portal shut again. "I'll report once we've checked the cabins and holds and everything's in order." Then the panels slid together and the bo'sun was gone.

"Always a pleasure, Kesselman," Demming muttered as he floated down the gangway, heading the length of the ship to engineering in the rear. "Don't ever change." Not that he disliked the bo'sun, particularly. But talking to him was always like speaking to a moderately clever child. The words were right, but he was never sure they really understood what he was saying.

Still, that wasn't his problem. And Kesselman did have the crew calm. That was the important thing.

Now to see what Amelia could tell him. Demming brightened at the thought of the pretty young engineer, and quickened his pace, speeding through the water.

"Took you long enough," Amelia groused when she irised the door open to engineering. But she'd answered immediately upon his knock, and there was a faint smile hovering on her lips, so Demming knew she wasn't too angry at him. Much.

"Sorry, I had to check on the crew first," he explained as he hauled himself into the engine room and glanced around. Normally there were at least three engineers on duty, and either Amelia or her second, Xander Twist, were with them. But during launch it was a good idea to keep the engineers close in case of trouble, so all fourteen of them were here. "Everyone okay?" he asked Amelia, focusing on two who were leaning over in their seats rather than checking equipment like everyone else.

"They're fine," she answered. "Roberts and Knightley took bumps to the head when we breached, but they're both okay, just a little woozy."

"Still, better to have Pasic check on them." Demming shoved down a surge of jealousy at the thought. Pasic could be Amelia's twin, tall and slender and good-looking, and the doctor was very smooth with the ladies. True, Amelia'd never shown any interest in him, but Demming hated throwing them together anyway. Still, the ship and her crew came first.

"Fair enough," Amelia agreed. She was good to her staff, Demming knew from watching her during leadership exercises. Not demanding enough, too willing to take on extra work herself instead of delegating it to others, but she didn't tolerate slackers, either. "So, what happened?"

"I was hoping you could tell me." Demming hooked one arm through a handhold and ran a hand over his head, the short dark hair there bristly beneath his touch. "We knew there'd be some sort of transition from air to ether, but that was a bit extreme! It threw everyone in the foredeck all about in their harnesses." He lowered his voice. "That's what did Holst in, I'm sure. Broke his neck when we hit . . . whatever we hit."

"Oh, poor Daniel!" Amelia's eyes got even wider and one hand flew to her mouth as her skin paled still more. "But we didn't hit anything," she continued a second later, visibly focusing on the problem instead of her grief. "The barrier . . . we'd always theorized that something had to be keeping the air in, beyond just it's being heavier than the ether beyond. There had to be more to it than that, some kind of shield or field or shell. And there was. That's what we went through. That's what tossed us about."

"All right, so it was exiting the air that was the problem, not entering the ether?"

"Exactly."

"And why're we stopped, then?"

The smile she gave him was wry and a little smug, but Demming thought he caught something else behind that. Just a flicker, but was that—fear?

"Who says we stopped?"

"The ship went dead," he pointed out. "Lights, impellers, everything. We slammed into the air's edge, or through it, and killed our momentum in the process." She was still smiling. "Didn't we?"

"The lights went dead, yes," Amelia agreed finally. "And the impellers stopped, too. Or rather they didn't have enough to work with, so they spun down to standby mode. But that doesn't mean we stopped moving."

Now Demming was confused. "How can we still be moving without the impellers?"

"See for yourself." Amelia glided over to one edge of the engineering compartment, beckoning for him to follow her. He was more than happy to oblige. All around them, the other engineers were taking readings and checking connections and scanning consoles, but they shifted to let the two of them float past.

Engineering was near the stern of the ship, between the impellers and just in front of the sonic pulse array. There was a rear hatch back here, and two small windows set by it, one to either side. Amelia led him to one of those and pushed upward to grasp a handhold set into the ceiling next to it. Demming did the same. Their faces were inches apart.

"Look," she told him softly, and it took some effort for Demming to tear his eyes off her luminous features and gaze upward instead. But when he did, he gasped.

"What is that?"

Beyond the portal, his eyes were met with a dazzling display. Back on the foredeck, Demming had thought the ether was dark as the abyss, but now it seemed he'd been wrong. Perhaps his eyes simply hadn't adjusted yet, or he'd been too shocked to register things clearly, or there had been something obstructing their view. But now he could see clearly, and what he saw was an amazing panoply of light. The ether was not a blank, featureless pale gray, as many had surmised. Instead it was jet black, blacker than black, but spotted throughout with pinpricks of white and red and pink and blue and other colors, some steady but many of them pulsing as if alive themselves. And mixed in with those, threaded among them and woven around them and floating beside them, were what looked almost like ink clouds, only these clouds were aburst with light and color, filled with a crimson glow or a rose one, a violet hue or an emerald haze. Many of those flickered as well, their colors shifting and changing as he watched. It was mesmerizing.

"This is amazing!" he whispered, and beside him Amelia nodded, so close the tip of her long braid brushed his shoulder. Then he remembered what she'd said before guiding him here. "But you said we were moving."

"Watch the lights," she instructed, and he did, concentrating on one pinprick and keeping his gaze locked there. He gasped again as it slid slowly down his field of view, until he lost it at the window's lower edge.

"We are moving! But how? The engines have no power, you said so yourself!"

"No, but we had a mighty push upon exiting the air," she reminded him. "We thought the same as you, at first—that the impact had stolen our momentum. Then we realized it hadn't. It just felt that way because we're moving without sound, without resistance, and without engines." She frowned. "Basically we're moving because we  were already in motion, and there's nothing to make us stop. Yet."

"And what happens when there is?" Demming asked. Normally their ships braked by reversing the impellers. That wouldn't work if the impellers had nothing to grab.

"I don't know," she admitted. "But we'll figure something out."

"I'm sure you will," he told her warmly. "What should I tell the captain, for now?" He didn't bother to mention that Mendez had been sedated last he'd seen. No sense worrying Amelia further.

"Tell her we're still underway, and in the right direction," Amelia answered. "And that we're working on sorting out navigation and steering."

Demming took one last look at the vibrant canopy beyond the window before releasing his handhold and letting the water pull him downward. "It wasn't supposed to be like this," he reminded her. "This isn't what the probes told us to expect." Four probes had been sent up before the *Remora* had launched, one of them before the ship's design had even been completed. The third probe had malfunctioned, but the other three had sent back data on the ether and what it contained. According to their readings, this space was supposed to be filled with boulders and rocks and strange cliffs and other objects, all packed as tightly together as a coral reef. In an environment like that, the *Remora*'s sonic pulses could be used to push off from each object, allowing them to maneuver through safely. But he hadn't seen anything solid out there, and those spots of light seemed awfully far away.

Amelia had dropped down alongside him. "I know—I'm still working on why the readings were so misleading." She gave him a smile, then, a smaller, sweeter smile than the amused almost-smirk she'd hit him with earlier. "Hey, it's an adventure, right?"

"Absolutely." He smiled back at her. "We wanted to explore the unknown, and we're certainly doing that!"

They both laughed a little nervously as they wove between engineers, back toward the door.

"I've got to get back and report," he explained as he cycled the door open. "I'm sure Captain Mendez will call a full meeting soon to go over things with everyone." He grinned. "And Quentin's already putting together a meal to tide us over."

That got a real laugh out of her. "Thank the wave! I'm starving!"

"I'll see you at the officer's mess, then," Demming told her as he floated back out into the gangway. "Buzz if anything comes up in the meantime."

"I will." She glanced down, and he thought he saw her cheeks flush before the door blocked her from view. Had she been blushing? He still couldn't read her properly.

But, he decided as he turned and swam back toward the foredeck, that was all right. He would just have to keep trying.

# CHAPTER SIX

"WELL." CAPTAIN MENDEZ LOOKED AROUND the table. They were gathered in the officers' mess, which doubled as the *Remora*'s conference room. "Not exactly how we expected, is it?"

That got a low chuckle, and Demming joined in. He'd been relieved to see the captain awake and calm, if still a bit pale beneath her olive complexion, when he'd returned to the foredeck. She'd taken charge again immediately, to Jacobsen's obvious relief—the acting first lieutenant still wasn't over his own shock, and had been delaying making any major decisions until absolutely necessary. That didn't necessarily bode well for how he'd handle himself if they did face a crisis, but right now Demming wasn't going to worry about that. He'd made his report to the captain, and she'd called a meeting immediately.

"First off," Mendez continued, "I want to think Mister Demming, Doctor Pasic, Mister Kesselman, and Miss Scutt for keeping their heads about them." She gave each of them an approving nod. "We were all a bit surprised by the . . . impact of our reaching the ether, and you four stayed calm and helped calm everyone else in turn. Well done." She glanced at the empty seat to her right. "As you have all heard by now, we have suffered a great loss. First Lieutenant Daniel Holst did not survive the transition from air to ether. Doctor Pasic assures me that he did not suffer, which is some comfort, at least." She paused a moment, and they all joined her in silence.

"We will hold a funeral service for Mister Holst as soon as it is practiceable," the captain assured them finally. "But for now we need to concentrate on getting ourselves and our ship back on course. To that end, I promote Mister Jacobsen to the post of First Lieutenant and Mister Demming to the position of Second Lieutenant, effective immediately." Everyone nodded, and Demming fought down the flush of pride as he saluted. Second Lieutenant! It was the position he'd wanted on the *Remora*, but he hadn't wanted to earn it like this.

"Mister Demming," Mendez addressed him, and he focused his attention back to the present.

"Yes, captain?"

"Are either of our two ensigns suited to take your place as Midshipman?"

Demming thought back to freeing himself and getting everyone moving. Both ensigns had been in shock, as had everyone else, but Pyle had stayed calmer and more focused. Craddick had curled in on himself and had to be snapped out of it. "Ensign Pyle, ma'am."

"Very good. After the meeting, please inform Midshipman Pyle of his promotion and instruct him in his new duties." The ensigns had been left to man the foredeck during the meeting.

"Aye aye, sir."

"Moving on," Mendez announced, rising to her feet and pacing along the front of the long table. "Miss Scutt!"

"Yes, ma'am?" It was clear that Amelia had been expecting this, and was already prepared to field the captain's questions.

"What exactly happened, Miss Scutt? Why did we experience such a violent entry to the ether?"

The captain already knew the answer to that, at least in brief, from Demming's own verbal report. She was asking in part to hear it in more detail and in part to make sure the other officers knew the answer as well—she was giving up a few minutes of her own time to help her officers become more informed, and to unite them further by hearing it with them. It was a smart tactic, and Demming filed the maneuver away for the distant future, when he would hopefully need such leadership skills himself.

Amelia launched into the same explanation she had given Demming earlier, about the barrier that held the air in around their world. When she was finished, the captain nodded.

"Then it is your opinion that we will not experience any more jolts like that one?"

"Not unless we encounter another world, captain," Amelia answered. She frowned, however. "There are some anomalies in our readings, however. The ether does not appear to be completely uniform. If we assume that it is similar in composition to water and air, only far more diffuse, we may encounter patches of heavier density and greater current. Those would produce some buffeting. But we should be able to see those coming."

"Which brings me to my next question." Mendez scowled, though she turned away from Amelia so the pretty young engineer would not think the expression was directed at her. Demming took note of that as well. "Why were the probes so sadly mistaken? We expected a boulder-strewn landscape, and instead we find"—she gestured at the porthole set in the mess's outer wall, which displayed the same light-filled panoply Amelia had shown Demming—"this."

"I have an answer for that, captain," Amelia assured her, setting both hands flat on the table, long fingers splayed against the smooth wood. "And it also explains why we are still moving, and at some speed, despite the impellers both being inactive." The captain nodded for her to continue. "When my team and I realized, from observing the stars, that we were still moving, we conducted several tests. The readings were . . . surprising, though in retrospect they should not have been. The clues were there all along, but no one was in a position to think them through." She shook her head, her long braid flying. "We knew that the ether would be lighter than air, and it is. What we failed to take into account was that it would also provide less resistance. Air has less resistance to water, and decreases still further as we go higher. It stands to reason, then, that ether would have even less resistance, or no resistance at all."

Mendez paused and gripped the back of her own chair with both hands, leaning against it. "And how does that explain the probes' incorrect readings?"

"They weren't incorrect," Amelia corrected. "We just didn't know how to read them properly." She rose as well, pushing back from the table and floating gracefully upward, gesturing with her hands to explain. "The probes used sonar to study the ether's topography, as usual. But sonar requires the sound waves to bounce off solid objects and return, thus forming a picture of those shapes. We can tell their distance by the strength of the returning signal, because the waves diminish as they travel further. But that's due to the resistance they receive in water or even air." She paused to make sure everyone was following her. "There's no resistance here! The sound waves traveled until they struck objects and then returned, regardless of the distance involved! That's why the probes thought there were reefs and boulders and other objects clustered together all around our world—those objects do exist, but they could be thousands of miles away, they were just the nearest shapes the sonar found!"

Demming thought about that, and nodded. It made sense. It was like line of sight—if you could see perfectly through a patch of water, you might see a ridge near you and another ridge a distance behind that one, and not realize the gap between them because they seemed equally close to your position. The sonar had overlapped the returning signals because there'd been no degradation, so the probes had assumed that meant all of the objects were equally close.

"And that's why we're moving without impellers?" Dittmer asked. "Because we were already moving when we breached the air, and without resistance there was nothing to slow us down?"

"Exactly!" Amelia's eyes shone. "We lost some momentum from the breach itself, and the impellers shut down because they had nothing to work with, so we all assumed that meant we'd stopped moving. But actually we only lost a fraction of our escape velocity—it's just that we're running without engines so we don't feel the motion. And without resistance, we could continue at this speed indefinitely!"

A few of the other officers nodded and even grinned, pleased at the thought of constant motion without a need for engines. But Demming frowned, and he saw Lizette, across from him, do the same.

"What happens when we need to slow down or stop?" The pretty pilot asked. "Or when we encounter some of those rocks we know are out there somewhere, and I have to steer us through them safely? We don't have the impellers to provide reverse thrust anymore!"

"That's not entirely true," Amelia argued. "The impellers have very little to work with out here—the ether's simply too thin for them to find any purchase. But we can override the normal intake activation control and switch them on manually—they won't have anything to grab, but the turbines will still spin, which will provide some current. It may not be enough for a quick stop, but it'll help slow us down."

Lizette was pondering that. "Will our maneuvering jets still work the same, then?" The *Remora*, like most ships, used jets of compressed air to steer. The small nozzles were placed all along the hull and linked together through the helm, so she could steer with the wheel and the appropriate jets would fire to turn the *Remora* in the right direction.

"They'll work far more efficiently, actually," Amelia warned. "You'll want to make only minute adjustments to our course— if you were to haul the wheel hard to starboard, you'd probably put the ship into a tailspin."

"Right, because no resistance means a single puff of air can turn us completely." Lizette nodded, her long hair bouncing from the motion. "I can work with that."

Demming had a question of his own. "What about the sonics, and the harpoons?" he asked. Amelia nodded, the slight smile that flickered across her face showing she knew where he was headed with this, but Molly beat her to the punch.

"All our weapons systems are functional," she answered, as usual her voice so low Demming had to strain to hear her. "They'll work fine without t resistance." He thought he saw a brief, sharp smile cross her lips, though it was hard to tell in the shadows of her curls. "In fact, I've got unlimited range now—I can hit anything we can pick up on sonar."

"That's good to know, thank you," Demming told her, "but

that wasn't exactly what I meant." He did address her with his next question, however, out of deference to her familiarity with the weapons. "The sonics have a small recoil when fired, correct?" She nodded. "And the harpoons as well?" Another nod, and he looked over at Amelia. "Would those recoils be enough to serve as a braking mechanism for the ship?"

The smile he got this time was full and bright. "I think so, yes. And between that and the impellers we should be able to stop the *Remora* fully, if necessary."

"Excellent news," Mendez commented, nodding her thanks to Amelia and sending the engineer drifting back down to her seat. "Thank you, Miss Scutt. And thank you, Miss Cuny, for confirming our weapons status. We've yet to see any signs of life here in the ether, but it never hurts to be prepared." She glanced at another officer, further down the table. "Speaking of prepared, Mister Dittmer, how stand our stores?"

"Excellent, captain," the quartermaster replied. "A few parcels were dented from the tumult, but nothing was broken. Everything's been restowed, and we're still at a full complement for food and water." A frown crossed his ruddy features, and Dittmer turned to Amelia. "Without the impellers, how do we stand for power? Will the scrubbers still be able to function properly?"

Amelia nodded, addressing her reply both to Dittmer and to the captain. "It's true that we would normally draw much of our energy from the impellers, but the rest comes from the ship's motion itself. We're currently traveling at greater speeds than we'd thought possible—I'd estimate roughly three thousand feet per second." Several people gasped at the figure, and Demming fought to restrain his own reaction. Three thousand feet per second! In open air the speed of sound was less than half that! Amelia allowed herself a brief smirk. "As you can imagine, given that velocity we've had no trouble keeping the ship's batteries charged."

"Which means, of course, that the scrubbers will function without any problem?" Mendez asked, and relaxed slightly at Amelia's nod. "Excellent, thank you, Miss Scutt." It was a huge relief. The scrubbers cleaned the water of waste, including carbon dioxide. The devices processed those waste gasses and converted them and other materials back to oxygen so that the crew could breathe. Before royal scientists had invented the scrubbers, they'd been restricted to using open-water vessels, which couldn't travel as fast, and closed ships that only went short distances.

"How are the crew holding up, Mister Kesselman?" the captain was asking, and Demming concentrated on the rest of the meeting even though he already knew the answer.

"Everyone is fine, Captain," the bo'sun replied. As always in the light his fine blond hair all but disappeared, making him appear bald, though that look worked with his strong features. "A few bumps and bruises but Doctor Pasic confirmed there was nothing worse, and after the initial panic I was able to restore calm. We swept the ship for any loose items, and made sure everything was stowed in its proper place again." He gave Demming a nod of thanks, and Demming thought he saw the captain arch an eyebrow slightly as she caught the silent exchange. Well, she knew Kesselman's abilities, so it shouldn't surprise her to learn that suggestion had come from him instead.

All she said, however, was "Good work, Mister Kesselman, thank you. Now that we know the ship is functional, and have a plan for continuing our mission, we'll return to active duty rosters and give the crew something to do." She smiled. "And

I believe Mister Watkins has already prepared a cold repast for us—since there seems to be no danger of running low on power or food, I'll give him the go-ahead to cook up something hot for supper later." Everyone visibly cheered at the thought, and Demming swallowed a laugh. It was amazing what the prospect of a hot meal could do for morale!

"Good job, everyone," Mendez told them, drifting back from the table and signaling that the meeting was at an end. "We've weathered our first crisis admirably, in no small measure due to your efforts, and I commend you all." She tapped the speaking tube control beside the door. "Mister Watkins, this is the captain—you can serve the food whenever you're ready."

As everyone shifted in their seats, Demming leaned across to speak with Amelia. "Nice work," he told her.

"You too. Thank you for mentioning the sonics and the harpoons. I'd forgotten to do so." She grinned for just a second, a quick flash of sunshine even in the brightly lit mess. "Though obviously Molly didn't."

He laughed with her. "No, she definitely didn't—I hope she didn't think I was intruding on her domain!" He cast a quick glance toward the tiny gunner's mate, briefly half-worried that she might launch an attack on him, but she was ignoring everyone else. As usual.

"I think you're safe for now," Amelia assured him, her laugh light and musical, obviously reading his nervous glance in that direction and well familiar with Molly's reputation. His joking reply was cut short by the sound of the door sliding open, to reveal Quentin and one of his assistants. Both men were laden with trays, and Demming rose to help them set those out on the table. There were salads and salted meats and wafers, nothing that had required cooking but filling nonetheless.

"What'd I miss?" Quentin asked quietly when Demming reached him, and Demming quickly caught him up on the contents of the meeting. "Well, congratulations, Second Lieutenant." The cook grinned and snapped off a quick salute. His grin faded to a genuine smile after a second, and he clapped Demming on the back. "You deserve it."

"Thanks." Demming returned to his seat, loading his plate with food, and as he ate he let his new rank sink in, finally. He hated that his promotion had come at the cost of Holst's life, but still it was nice to be recognized for his efforts, and to attain the higher rank.

He just hoped that was the only promotion he would receive during the course of their mission.

# CHAPTER SEVEN

THEY WERE STILL PICKING AT the remains of the meal, almost an hour later, when the door chimed. Jacobsen was closest to it, and he drifted off and hit the speaker.

"Yes?"

Demming couldn't hear the reply, but he saw the newly minted first lieutenant frown. "Miss Scutt?"

Amelia gave Demming an apologetic half-smile—they'd been chatting quietly—and floated over to the door. It whisked open, and beyond it Demming could just make out a short, blocky figure. That would make it her engineer's mate, Xander Twist. They conversed for a moment, then Amelia turned back toward the other officers.

"Captain? Miss Mills? You'll want to hear this."

That got everyone's attention, and Amelia noticed it. She raised her voice to make sure everyone could hear her. "Xander tells me we're rapidly approaching a collection of rocks and boulders in the ether." She smiled. "We'd had some ideas on how to recalibrate the sonar, which I didn't want to mention until we'd tested them. It looks like they've worked. We're using the time lag from the signal's departure to its return to measure distance, so now we can actually gauge distance properly."

"Good work, Miss Scutt," Mendez complimented. "Very well—Miss Mills, are you ready to test the *Remora*'s braking and maneuvering capabilities in ether?"

Lizette grinned, the smile lighting her face. There was a reason most of the male officers flirted with her. "Absolutely, captain!" She slipped past Amelia and Twist and Jacobsen and swam quickly toward the foredeck, vanishing from view as she headed down the gangway. Demming was already out of his chair, wiping at his mouth with his napkin before tossing that onto his plate and adding them both to the basin for dirty dishes.

"Permission to stand on the foredeck, captain?" he asked as he neared Mendez. Off to the side he saw Jacobsen scowl, and hid a grin. Except during combat or launch, it was customary to avoid having both lieutenants on the foredeck—that way, if anything happened the entire command structure would not be wiped out at once. Since he'd asked first, if the captain approved it meant Jacobsen couldn't watch the maneuvers from there. But that was the price he paid for not acting more quickly.

Mendez apparently agreed. "Permission granted, Mister Demming." The glint in her eye said she completely understood what he'd just done. "I believe I'll amble that way myself." She passed through the still-open doorway and Demming fell into kick beside her, giving Amelia a quick wave good-bye as he passed. She nodded. One of the drawbacks to her being the chief engineer was that she needed to be down in the engine room during most of their critical maneuvers. They had their two small ports, of course, but it wasn't the same as watching from the foredeck. It also meant that she and Demming would be at opposite ends of the ship.

But that didn't stop him from looking forward to the

encounter they were about to experience.

Lizette had already replaced Pyle behind the wheel by the time Demming and the captain arrived. Mendez immediately took her seat, but Demming paused to corner Pyle.

"Everything okay up here, Mister Pyle?" he asked quietly. Lizette was eyeing the ether in front of them, and he didn't want to distract her. It had sounded like they could hit those rocks at any time.

"Fine, sir," Pyle answered. "Miss Mills just relieved me."

"Very good." Demming paused. "You handled the breach well, Mister Pyle. The captain agrees. With Mister Holst lost to us, Jacobsen has been promoted to first lieutenant, and I've taken his old post as second lieutenant." He still got a thrill saying that. "The captain asked for my recommendation for midshipman, and I selected you."

Pyle's eyes got wide, but he didn't gasp or stutter. Instead, after an instant of shock, he straightened and saluted. "Yes, sir! Thank you, sir!"

"You're welcome. I'll brief you on your new duties, of course, but for now it sounds like we're in for a show." Demming clasped the new midshipman's hand, then drifted past him and took the seat in front of his old one. The second lieutenant's chair. He had an unobstructed view out the front canopy, and he settled into his seat to watch and wait.

As it turned out, the wait was short. After a few minutes his eyes adjusted to the flickering lights and strangely lit clouds and pulsating pinpricks that filled the ether, and Demming began to pick out actual features. There, they had just passed a burning globe like their sun but far, far larger and of a deeper, angrier hue. Just beyond that were a handful of smaller globes, none of them lit from within but a few reflecting the light of their sun or capturing it within wisps of cloud cover. Over there, beyond that cluster, was a loose strand of rocks, stretched out through the ether like a school of fish. He had the impression that those rocks were farther and larger than he realized—it was still hard to reconcile there being no distortion over distance here, so everything was as clear at the edge of his sight as it was nearby—but there were many small specks he suspected were rocks no larger than the *Remora,* and possibly as small as a waveglider or kickboard. Then his attention fixed on a handful of specks directly ahead.

"Miss Mills," he started, but her nod and the flick of her long hair cut him off.

"I see them, Mister Demming," she responded. "Thank you." She gave him a quick grin over her shoulder to show she wasn't angry at him, only focused. Of course she had sharp eyes—that, fast reflexes, and a natural touch with the wheel were what had earned her the pilot's berth.

Within minutes the others had spied the rocks as well, or had them pointed out. And the rocks were definitely growing larger. Demming remembered again the speed Amelia had estimated. Three thousand feet per second! It had been at least three minutes since he'd spotted the boulders, which meant they'd covered roughly over half a million feet in that time. And the rocks were still some distance away, assuming they were large enough to pose a threat to the ship. Astounding!

Two more minutes and the rocks had grown to the size of a man's head in their view.

"We should be on them in two more minutes," Lizette announced to the others. "Miss Scutt has patched her modified sonar view to my console, and I've already plotted a course through the obstacle field. There hasn't been time to fix the impellers yet, so I'm firing the forward maneuvering jets to slow us a little." Demming let out his breath. He'd been afraid she was going to try steering them through those boulders at their current speed! Lizette was a fine pilot, and like most pilots she loved to go fast, but navigating through a field of rock at twice the speed of sound? Not the best idea for their first day in the ether.

"Everyone to their harnesses, please," Captain Mendez announced. She sounded completely calm. "Let's play this one safe, shall we?"

Demming buckled his harness into place, and heard muted clicks as the others around the room did the same. Besides him and the captain and Lizette, Pyle and Craddick were still here and Doctor Pasic had joined them. Mister Dittmer must have stayed in the officer's mess, or perhaps gone to the crew quarters or even the stores. And of course Jacobsen would be in the mess or the crew quarters as well. For a brief instant Demming worried that the charming first lieutenant had followed Amelia back to engineering, but brushed the thought aside. She'd never shown any interest in Jacobsen. Besides, engineering would be a tense place right now, and not one anyone would choose to visit during this little maneuver.

The boulders now seemed as large as a man, and they were visibly expanding. He could make out some details to them now. They were irregularly shaped, with jagged edges and mottled surfaces, mostly blacks and grays and browns but with sparks of brighter color here and there like precious stones peeking up from a bed of black sand. The rocks weren't solid masses, either—in several places he saw loops and arcs of stone sweeping out from a central form, much like the waves carved places through coral and rock back home. The familiarity of those shapes struck Demming with a sudden wave of homesickness, which he pushed back down. Now was no time for such distractions.

"Prepare for evasive maneuvering," Lizette declared. She'd donned her harness as well, but because she needed to stand to operate the wheel her harness was built off the low rail in front of her instead of a seat. That was the price one paid for being the pilot—when you were on duty you didn't get to sit down.

Demming braced himself, gripping his armrests, and was amused to notice there were still indentations there from the chair's previous occupant. Jacobsen had clearly been petrified.

Then the first of the rocks was before them, suddenly looming up to fill the canopy. Lizette flicked the wheel a fraction to the right, and Demming could feel a faint shudder from his side of the ship as the *Remora*'s maneuvering jets fired along the left side, angling the ship to the right. Her nose slid past the massive boulder, which now seemed more like a jagged cliff suspended in the inky darkness of the ether, and he stared at the rough, pitted surface as they swept past. What had struck this slab of stone to cause such deep furrows and scrapes? Other rocks? Or were there other things out here in the ether that had slammed full-force into the monolith?

A second expanse lurched toward them, and Lizette tugged back on the wheel, raising the *Remora*'s prow to point it through the hole that gouged straight through the floating mountain. They soared cleanly through that uneven gap, and immediately tilted back down to avoid the sharp edges of a small rock that floated in the first one's wake.

Lizette handled the field deftly, slipping left and right, sliding up and down, twisting the ship so her impellers squeaked down narrow cracks between two slabs or glided just above a long, smooth expanse of stone like the ocean floor. With the rocks zooming past all around them Demming could better gauge their speed, and even after braking it was immense. He was sure no one had ever traveled at such a velocity before, and the idea of how far they had already traveled left him slightly dizzy. There were a few close calls, mainly where the sonar had not been able to register a second rock behind a first one, but Lizette compensated quickly and an hour after they'd reached the cluster she skirted the last boulder and they were sailing through empty ether once more.

"Beautifully handled, Miss Mills," the captain told her warmly. "An exceptional job, and I'd say our jets handled perfectly."

"Thank you, captain." Lizette all but glowed at the compliment. "And yes, the *Remora* responded well. Miss Scutt was absolutely right—I only needed the lightest touch to make her leap in whatever direction I desired."

Demming unfastened his harness and rose, kicking softly to bring him closer to the captain's chair. "A question, captain?"

"Yes, Mister Demming?" She turned to regard him, still sitting back and looking very much in command.

"The light that first launched us on this mission, captain—I know the royal scientists studied it as best they could, and marked its position in the ether." He paused as she nodded. "But with Miss Scutt's new modifications, is there any way to determine just how far we might be from its position? If so, we could calculate how long the trip might take, and compare that to our stores to see if we needed to ration our usage more strictly."

"An excellent point, Mister Demming." The captain gave him an approving nod, then tapped the speaking-tube controls on her chair. "Miss Scutt, this is the captain."

"Yes, captain?" Amelia replied after a moment.

"Miss Scutt, would it be possible to determine our distance to the light we spied through the water those many months ago?"

There was a longer pause. "I'm not sure, captain. We aren't seeing the light anymore, so I can't track it with the *Remora*'s sonar. I do have the readings the royal scientists took at the time, and I may be able to enter those into our systems to see if we can analyze their sonar imprints, but it will take some time."

"Understood. Do what you can. We may need to know how much farther we have to travel." The captain closed the connection and turned back to Demming. "We'll find some way to answer your question, Mister Demming," she assured him. "I agree, it could prove very important to know how many meals we must allot for the voyage out, to speak nothing of the trip back home."

The trip back home. That thought burst into Demming's head as he saluted and glided back to his chair. He'd been so caught up in their launch, and then the excitement and oddity of the ether, that he hadn't given any consideration to the second half of their mission—to find out about the light and return with news of its origins. But how?

That question gave him a sudden chill, which he tried to disguise by shifting his weight in his seat. They had launched from the water, and added sonic pulses to boost them through the air, which had led to their speed when they'd breached the air. Out here they were still moving at the same speed, or a little less now after Lizette's braking. But that was because they were continuing in the same direction. If they came to a stop, how would they ever get started again? And if they tried to turn around, how much of their momentum would they shed from reversing their course? Would they have enough velocity left to make their way home once more?

For that matter, would they even be able to find their way home? Where there any shapes they could identify out there, that they could use as signposts? Already they'd covered several million feet. Their home was long since beyond even the sharpest eyes. If the light was millions or billions or even trillions of feet farther, how would they know the correct direction when they ventured back? Without a proper bearing, they could be lost in the ether forever!

# CHAPTER EIGHT

"HERE WE GO AGAIN," PYLE muttered as he strapped in. Demming smiled. This was the fourth etheric atoll they'd encountered since the *Remora*'s launch, and the new midshipman had taken advantage of his increased rank to be in the foredeck for each and every one. But the nonchalance was completely faked, and Demming knew if he were to crane his neck to peek over his chair he'd see the younger officer sitting there, hands tight on the armrests, eyes wide, with a huge grin plastered across his face.

Nor could Demming blame him. He'd missed the last two rings of stone, since Jacobsen had insisted on taking both of those, and was looking forward to watching Lizette navigate this one. Observing it from one of the small portholes in the officer's mess just wasn't the same.

"Time to the atoll is two minutes," Lizette called from the wheel. As usual she sounded excited but calm. She'd been flushed after navigating the first atoll, and if not for Mendez's strict orders about fraternizing Demming suspected the curvy little pilot would have found a partner to help her release some of that enthusiasm. Plenty of the crew—and most of the officers—would have been more than willing to join her. He would have regretfully declined, himself, but only because he was afraid doing anything with Lizette would hurt his chances with Amelia.

As it was, the captain frowned heavily upon such assignations while onboard, so Lizette had been forced to content herself with sparring in the gymnasium. She'd been exhausted, exhilarated, and sheened in sweat when she'd finished, her long silk hair coming loose from the topknot she'd set it in, and behind her a handful of men and women had groaned at her departure, but not in the usual fashion. Demming had been among that group, and it had felt good to work out the kinks left over from their explosive exit launch.

Since then, the ship had settled into a nice, steady routine. Pyle had taken to the midshipman's duties quickly and easily, and had proven adept at relaying messages and facilitating communication between the commanding officers, the bo'sun, the mates, and the rest of the crew. Demming had adjusted to his own new role, which was in some ways far less active than his old one. Part of that was because Jacobsen acted like a man who had something to prove. The new first lieutenant was everywhere for the first week, involving himself in every aspect of operations and daily activity. Since the second lieutenant's job was to provide support for the first lieutenant and the captain, that left Demming at loose ends most of the time. He wound up being confined to the foredeck for most of his active duty, because Jacobsen was swimming through this compartment or that, demanding on-the-spot reports from engineering, stores, weapons, and the galley.

"He's gone mad with power," Amelia had told Demming quietly one morning when they'd actually chanced to be in the officers' mess together. He'd barely seen her that week, except for at the evening meal. Captain Mendez was old-fashioned enough to insist that the entire officers' complement, save those actively on watch, sat dinner together every night. Demming actually appreciated that. It was a nice way to round out the day, and to foster a connection among them. But of course conversation was limited during those meals, especially if it involved one of the others present.

"He may feel guilty for how he got the rank," Demming had pointed out, slathering a piece of bread with preserves. "I know I do."

"Maybe, but I don't think that's all of it." She had stirred her tea and took another sip. "He's always been a little full of himself, but I think the new rank has gone to his head. He acts like he's the only officer onboard, and expects to be kept abreast of everything everyone does." A grimace had crossed her face. "He actually wanted me to notify him every time the scrubbers ran through their cleaning cycle!"

Demming had laughed at that. "You should take him at his word, then! Notify him every time that happens!" He knew, from one unfortunate training run where he'd been assigned to assist the engineer with repairing a damaged scrubber that they cycled every five minutes. No matter what. They'd had to time their repairs to take advantage of the gaps in that schedule, fixing the problem in stages, and it had taken over three hours to make a repair that should have taken only forty minutes!

Fortunately Jacobsen had calmed down a little since then. He was still full of himself, of course, and still swam around as if he owned the ship, but he'd stopped demanding to know everything that went on in every nook and cranny. And he'd started letting Demming handle some of the lieutenant duties as well. Not enough, perhaps, but at least some.

Amelia and her team had reconfigured the impellers as promised, and were able to give Lizette a bit more braking power, as well as a way to boost the *Remora* back up to mind-boggling speeds once they were clear of any obstacles or terrain.

Pasic had checked everyone and confirmed that no one had any significant injuries. All bruises and scrapes had long since healed by now.

They were still working on a way to measure the distance to the light source, so until then the captain had put the ship on a moderate rationing schedule. Quentin was a master at stretching out food supplies, fortunately, so if the meals were a little less lavish than before no one noticed.

The crew had also settled into their routines. Kesselman made sure every surface was kept clean and clear, in part because both he and the captain liked a clean ship and in part because it kept the crew busy. They took readings for the engineers, rotated kitchen duties under Quentin's sharp eye, exercised and worked out, ran the occasional drill, and otherwise played cards, diced, read, wrote, sparred, and passed the time. As Demming's grandfather had warned him long ago "life on a ship is long stretches of boredom, interspersed with moments of frantic excitement."

Wending their way through an atoll was always one of the latter, however, and Demming felt his pulse race as he waited eagerly for this cluster of rocks to arrive.

"Braking," Lizette declared, hand on the throttle, and Demming felt the ship shudder as the impellers fired. True to Amelia's word, they slowed the ship from breakneck speed to simply heart-wrenching. He knew from the grin he saw on the pilot's face that she wouldn't want to loose any more speed than she had to.

The first row of boulders loomed up around them, darker and more blue-black than the set Demming had seen the first time, and Lizette's other hand tapped the wheel, spinning the *Remora* lightly to one side of the massive cliff before them. She dodged a second expanse, slipped beneath a third, and curved past a fourth so closely Demming thought he could have run his fingers across its pitted surface if their canopy had been open.

She was just twisting the wheel to aim for a gap between two more when something glittering and blue flashed toward them from that same narrow space.

"What—?" Demming's eyes flicked to his console, and what he saw there stole his voice for half a second. Then he regained it to shout, "Incoming!"

Lizette reacted immediately. She slammed down on the throttle, the impellers firing full-force as she tried to stop the *Remora* cold. They were moving too fast for that, however, and whatever that glowing shape was, it was heading straight for them! But Lizette was spinning the wheel at the same time—she converted some of the *Remora*'s momentum into a vicious roll that spun the entire ship along its axis, and even after shedding that much velocity they still had enough speed to dart left, away from what Demming's eyes had registered as a blinding afterimage—and a disturbingly familiar shape.

A net.

"Miss Cuny! Battle stations!" The captain roared from her chair, and Demming was sure the tiny gunner's mate was already racing toward the weapons deck, if she wasn't there already. "Miss Mills, get us out here! All officers and crew, prepare for possible ship-to-ship combat!"

"Combat?" Demming heard Pyle whisper behind him. "With whom?"

Which was a very good question.

And one it looked like they might have to answer, as a second net blossomed in their new path. Lizette angled the *Remora* below it, but the net changed its course and followed them downward, its strands an electric blue against the dark rocks and the darker ether. A chilling thought hit Demming, and he studied his console's monitor again. What he saw there confirmed his fears.

"The other net!" he shouted. "It's following us! It must be magnetized!"

"Impossible!" Dittmer argued from his own station. "The rocks around us—"

"—are nonmagnetic!" Demming interrupted. "That's why whoever's here chose this spot! They knew our ship was metal and the rocks weren't, so the nets would go right for us!"

Though that still begged the question—who could possibly be out here? And how could they know anything about the *Remora*?

There was no question, though, that there was someone. These were nets. They'd been crafted. And whoever it was had laid an ambush here, right where the *Remora* would pass by.

Deal with the who and the why later, Demming reminded himself. Deal with the how and the how to get out of it now.

But it didn't seem like that latter was going to happen. There was a sudden lurch from the *Remora*'s rear, and then the ship seemed to shudder. And slow. "The first net's caught us!" Lizette confirmed. "And we're losing speed!"

"Captain!" That was Amelia through the speaking-tube. "Whatever this net is, it's draining the ship's power! Our batteries are down to half already!"

Lizette cried out, and Demming's eyes flicked back up to

her, and to the windows beyond her. Glittering blue strands filled his view, and when the ship shook again he knew the second net had caught them from the front. Beyond those glowing constraints he could see the lights of the ether slow to a crawl and then a standstill, at the same time as the rocks all around them stopped sliding past and simply towered up on every side.

"We're at a full stop!" Lizette announced. "No motion at all!"

"Ship's down to ten percent power," Amelia added from engineering. "If we drop below five we won't have enough to operate the scrubbers!"

"Captain!" That was Molly Cuny, over the speaking-tube. "We've got another ship approaching!"

Mendez was out of her harness and out of her seat in an instant. Demming had never seen the captain so energized—or so angry. Her olive skin was flushed, and her heavy face set in a deep, fierce scowl. "Where?" she demanded.

"Hard to starboard, approaching from the rear," the gunner's mate reported. "Unfamiliar configuration but comparable size to the *Remora*. Shall I fire on them?" For once she wasn't whispering—her words were crisp and clear, and there was a dreadful eagerness in them.

Mendez paused for a second. At first Demming couldn't understand why. They'd just been ambushed, completely becalmed, and now they were clearly about to be boarded! Of course they should fight back! But as he thought about it, he understood the captain's thinking. Right now they were helpless. Whoever this was, they could probably overpower the crew. Unless Molly could destroy or at least disable the other ship before it could reach the *Remora*, attacking now would only anger them.

Sure enough, the captain's next words were a question. "What is your opinion, Miss Cuny? Can you take them out?"

This time it was the gunner's mate who paused. Finally she admitted, "No, captain. I can't guarantee the sonic lance's effectiveness in ether, or the sonic ram's, and they look to be heavily armored." It was obvious from her tone that she hated having to give that answer.

So did Mendez, judging by her sigh and the way her shoulders slumped. "Very well. Stand down, Miss Cuny. Let's not give them an excuse, shall we?"

Demming swallowed hard. "What are your orders, captain?" he asked finally. He had a sinking feeling he already knew the answer.

He was right. "Stand down, Mister Demming," she confirmed, returning to her seat and dropping heavily into it. "A fight right now would only put us in a worse position. Let's hope whoever has waylaid us is reasonable, and sees that we are not putting up opposition."

Let's hope, Demming agreed privately. But he had a sinking suspicion their ambushers would not prove so civilized.

# CHAPTER NINE

"I HATE THIS," DEMMING MUTTERED softly, pounding one fist upon his chair.

Apparently not softly enough, however, because the captain glanced over at him. "So do I, Mister Demming," she replied quietly. "So do I." Her own hands lay folded in her lap. "But I have to put the ship and her crew first, and sometimes that means making unpleasant decisions, decisions that go against every grain, even against my sense of honor or right. That is the burden of command."

Demming nodded. He knew that, of course, but he'd never had to put it in practice before. Nor had he ever seen it exercised so fully. In Mendez's place, he knew he probably would have fought regardless. But that would have angered their ambushers, and most likely gotten some of the crew injured or even killed. Worse, their attackers could have chosen to take out the *Remora* herself, thus dooming everyone onboard. Was that risk worth assuaging his feelings of helplessness, or his wounded pride? He'd known from watching her that Captain Mendez was not the most . . . aggressive of commanders, but she had probably made the right choice. In her shoes, he wasn't sure he could have done the same.

Which didn't make him hate their helplessness any less.

"Ship within a hundred feet, Captain," Lizette warned, and Demming glanced at his own monitor, calling up the image from the pilot's scope. And gasped. He had never seen anything like what was now approaching them.

He could only see it as a sonar reading, of course, but even so! It was . . . monstrous!

Every ship in the Royal Navy was sleek and swift and streamlined like the sea creatures that darted around them. This new ship was awkward and ungainly, with hard, stiff lines and strange jutting shapes. It resembled a crab more than anything, particularly what looked like claws off to the sides and what resembled pincers or feelers out in front of the narrowing prow. He supposed it didn't have to be sleek out here in the ether, where there was no resistance to overcome from the thin substance. A ship could be round or even square and still move effectively. But why would anyone want a ship like that?

"Attention, all crew," Captain Mendez announced over the speaking tubes. "We are about to be boarded. Offer no resistance. I repeat, offer no resistance. Behave courteously, obey any orders, and keep your tongues. That is all."

She straightened in her chair and swiveled it around to face the others on the foredeck. "This is a historic occasion, ladies and gentlemen," she informed them, a weak smile touching her lips. "We had thought the *Remora* was the first ship of any sort to breach the air and travel the ether. Clearly we were wrong. But since we know no other ship has ever traveled from our world, we must assume this approaching vessel is from elsewhere. That means we are the first people to meet travelers from another world." She tugged at her uniform's front, and swept a wayward hair back from her forehead. "Let us behave with the decorum and civility appropriate to the occasion."

Let us hope our visitors do the same," Demming thought grimly. But he did not say that. He had his orders, and speaking out would serve no purpose except to annoy his captain and increase the tension already thick on the foredeck. Nonetheless, he checked that his diving knife was still secure in his boot, and relaxed slightly as the carved bone handle pressed against his calf.

"Ship about to make contact," Lizette reported. A shudder ran the length of the *Remora*, accompanied by the hollow clang of metal on metal. "Contact."

"Captain!" That was Amelia over the speaking tubes, and Demming's heart clenched. "They're over our rear port! It looks like they're attempting a seal!"

That made sense, of course. They had no idea what the ether itself was like—the *Remora*'s external sensors had not been able to pick up any effective readings due to the speed they'd possessed since their launch—but most likely it was not hospitable. The safest course to travel ship-to-ship was to seal the ports together, locking out the ether and anything else that might float out there. They'd have used the same technique underwater, especially in the deeps where maintaining the ships' pressure was potentially crucial.

"Allow the seal," Miss Scutt," Mendez answered. "Keep your team clear, and make no hostile moves."

"Yes, sir." Amelia severed the connection, and Demming clenched his jaw at the futility he could hear in her quiet tone. He hoped the captain was right. He hoped they would all be okay. Especially Amelia. She and her engineers were the first ones these strangers would encounter. If the captain was wrong about their disposition, it was the engineers who would pay the price.

Another, softer clang indicated that the ports had been lined up and connected. "Seal has been achieved," Lizette informed the room. "Pressures equalized." She frowned, studying her readouts. "Actually, no—the other ship's pressure is half a measure less than ours."

Less? Demming glanced at the captain, who looked equally puzzled. Why would they keep the pressures separate? Then he realized. If the other ship had less pressure, it would prevent the *Remora*'s atmosphere from leaking through the seal. The heavier pressure here would hold their water down on their side, allowing the strangers to enter and exit without carrying the liquid with them. It was an interesting precaution, and one that both impressed him and worried him. Who were these people that they considered the possibility that the *Remora*'s atmosphere might be hostile to them?

"Ship's rear port has been accessed," Lizette announced. "They are entering the *Remora*."

All sound on the foredeck ceased. Demming saw he was not alone in leaning forward, straining to hear any sound that might carry down the gangway from engineering.

He thought he heard something after a few seconds. A soft *whump* like a gasp for breath, or a heavy boot settling to the floor. A second, similar *thump* followed a moment later, and he thought he felt a faint tremor through the floor. But if that second sound had been something dropping, what was the first?

"They've accessed the main gangway," was Lizette's next report. "They're heading this way."

Captain Mendez nodded and rose to her feet. "Prepare to greet our guests," she informed the room, and her officers stood after her.

Demming was glad to be on his feet again. At least it felt less passive than sitting quietly, awaiting their fate. It did mean his knife was out of quick reach, however. He hoped that wouldn't prove to be a bad choice.

He could hear sounds from the gangway now, the heavy thud of feet marching toward the foredeck. Why weren't they swimming, he wondered. It was faster and easier. But perhaps the strangers were not as comfortable out of contact with the ground. That made him feel a little better.

As he listened, something else nagged at him. There was something strange about the approaching rhythm. He had done plenty of marching as a cadet—it was supposed to strengthen certain leg muscles they didn't use as heavily when swimming, and to prepare them in case of a hull breach or one of the rare, risky missions to those isolated outcroppings of land above the water's surface. The beat of feet upon a deck was one he'd heard many times, and he had learned to appreciate it because it allowed him to move his own body in time and thus stay in formation with the others. But this? This was different. There was something wrong with the sound. The beat was off.

He wondered what that meant.

Well, he would find out soon enough.

It seemed like hours before they heard the oddly off-kilter rhythm stop just beyond the foredeck's door. There was a pause, and then the porthole irised open. Several short, ungainly figures stepped over the lower lip and entered the command cabin.

Demming gaped, and had to stop himself from sputtering up water like a child. He heard similar reactions around him, and Pyle did choke slightly, though the young midshipman managed to control himself quickly. All of them stared, however.

And with good reason.

Demming realized that he had simply assumed these strangers would be like them. From another world, yes, but otherwise the same. Instead, he found himself facing creatures he had never even imagined.

Like their ship, these strangers were awkward and ungainly. No taller than Lizette, they were broader than Dittmer or Kesselman, with blocky torsos and wide hips. That was apparently necessary to accommodate the additional arm and extra leg they bore. For these strangers were not bipedal, as all humans were. They were tripedal instead, their three short, thick legs ranged equally around their body below three powerful arms. No wonder the rhythm had seemed off!

Demming could not see their faces, though he assumed those would be equally strange. Did they have three eyes as well, he wondered? The answer was unclear because the strangers were wearing what looked much like deep-sea diving suits, heavily armored and segmented to allow easy movement. Bulky gloves tapered down to surprisingly delicate fingers, and massive boots clearly weighed them down so they could cling to the deck. Strange helmets covered their heads, conical affairs with a ring of what appeared to be dark glass circling at what Demming assumed was eye height. It appeared his guess about a third eye was correct.

Something else quickly drew his attention, however. Actually, two things. The first was Amelia. The strangers had dragged her with them, one on either side holding her tight between them, and now they flung her to floor before their feet. She had a bruise across one cheek, the sight of which made Demming see red, and was sobbing slightly, but looked otherwise unharmed.

The other thing, however, made Demming's blood go cold. The strangers bore guns.

Weapons weren't common onboard a ship. They had a few handheld harpoons, of course, and a few sonic rifles. But they were rarely needed. Most pirates knew to flee when a ship of the Royal Navy appeared, and those foolish enough to stand and fight were quickly disabled by sonic lances and sonic rams and ship-mounted harpoons and electrified nets. Only the most foolhardy pirates put up resistance after their ship had been disabled. It was incredibly rare for a member of the navy to experience combat in person.

These odd, armored figures looked comfortable bearing arms, however. Too comfortable. Demming didn't recognize the design—the weapons were handheld, pistols rather than rifles, but long and bulky and angular. They looked ugly and effective. He hoped the creatures would not have an excuse to use them.

The stranger in front had been scanning the foredeck while Demming and the others had studied him and his companions. Now he strode across to where Captain Mendez waited, floating calmly in front of her chair. "You!" The stranger's voice was rough and raspy, the single word harshly accented. "You are in charge?"

She nodded. "I am Hardesty Mendez, captain of the HMES *Remora*. Might I have the pleasure of your name?"

That gave him—from the deep voice Demming guessed the stranger was male—pause. Finally he replied. "Suwa Jem." He thumped a heavy hand against his armored chest. "Captain of the *Siren Knife*. We have taken your ship." Suwa Jem studied the assemblage again. "These are your officers?"

"Yes." Mendez kept her face and voice calm. "What are

your intentions toward us, Captain Jem? You notice that we are cooperating. We do not wish for any trouble."

The creature chuckled, his body shaking with the deep, chilling sound. "Our intentions? We mean to rob you, Captain Mendez! That is what space pirates do!"

Space pirates? The words hit Demming like a blow, and he saw Mendez and several of the others reel at the blunt statement as well. They had never expected something like this!

"This entire ship"—Suwa Jem gestured with one hand, taking in the cabin around them—"is like this?" Mendez frowned. "Filled with this?"

"With water?" She nodded. "Yes. We live in water. You do not?"

The pirate captain didn't bother to answer. Instead he glanced back at one of his own crew. "Ready the pumps," he ordered, and the creature nodded. One of the heavy gloves had a strange control panel on its back, and the pirate tapped several buttons there in rapid sequence, then began speaking swiftly. Demming couldn't make out the words, or even if they were familiar, but he assumed the pirate was conveying his captain's orders.

"What else?" Suwa Jem demanded. "Show me."

Mendez glanced over at Dittmer and nodded. The quartermaster tapped a command into his screen, then swiveled the display toward the pirate captain. "Our inventory," he explained as the strange creature stomped forward and shouldered him aside to study the list. "Located in the cargo holds to the rear."

Suwa Jem nodded, and gestured to one of his other men. "Strip the holds." The pirate marched off, his movements stiff and ungainly in the water. "Weapons?"

"We are an exploratory vessel," Mendez replied, drawing the pirate's attention back to her. Demming tensed. Now was the time to act. Suwa Jem had sent one of his crew away, and the first one had turned and departed as well, no doubt to supervise the pumps that would steal their water. That left the pirate captain with only two others. They could overpower him, take his weapons, and then surprise the other two by the port and the hold. Then they could reseal the rear portal, push off from the other ship—Suwa Jem had called it the *Siren Knife*— and take off. Possibly even disable the pirate ship with the sonic ram, at least long enough to escape among the rocks of the atoll.

But Mendez noticed his posture and ever so faintly shook her head. By the abyss! Demming considered disobeying, but wasn't sure the other officers would follow suit. He forced himself to relax and straighten to full attention again.

"We have very little in the way of armaments," Mendez continued, her calm tone giving no indication that she had just shut down a potential counterattack. "We have a harpoon and a sonic lance to repel any potential threats, but those are suited only to marine creatures or their etheric equivalent."

The pirate captain snorted. "Those are useless," he confirmed. "Won't pierce ship plating." His helmet swiveled up and down slightly as he studied the *Remora* captain. "No personal weapons?"

"We have no need for them," Mendez answered. Of course there was a cache of sonic rifles, cutlasses, belaying pins, and clubs stowed in a secure compartment within the foredeck's wall, and a similar but larger collection in the crew quarters, but clearly she saw no reason to mention those. And it seemed that the *Siren Knife* lacked the ability to scan the *Remora*'s interior properly, else they would not have needed to ask about the ship's stores.

A grinding noise began, somewhere near the ship's rear, and Mendez started slightly. So did Demming. Suwa Jem didn't budge, however. After a second Demming felt a shift in the current, and saw water beginning to swirl through the foredeck's door, which was still open. They had begun the pumps!

Another tremor shivered the ship, and he guessed that was the feel of the cargo holds being opened and emptied.

One of the other pirates—Demming suspected it was the one who'd been ordered to man the pumps—returned and clomped over to Suwa Jem. "Liquid secured in four clicks," he reported shortly. "Holds in two." His helmet shifted toward Mendez, Dittmer, and the rest. "Them?"

That got another snort from his captain. "Not enough value to justify passage," Suwa Jem answered, and Demming shivered as he realized they were discussing the question of selling the crew! Slavery had been outlawed for generations on their world, but there were histories of a time when it had occurred and pirates had trafficked in human lives as well as food, weapons, and goods. Clearly such barbarism was still the case out here!

"Back to the *Siren Knife* when this is empty," Suwa Jem ordered, and his three crewmen nodded behind him. Demming felt a chill ruffle his hair, and realized that the water was receding rapidly. Already it lapped a foot or more below the cabin's ceiling. It was amazing that the other ship could drain the *Remora*'s water that quickly, and he marveled at the power of their pumps even as he worried about the consequences.

Apparently he wasn't the only one. "You can't take our water!" Captain Mendez insisted, stepping closer to Suwa Jem and resting a hand on the pirate captain's arm. "We need it to survive!"

"Not my problem." He shrugged off her hand. Then he stepped back a pace and studied her. The water had now dropped to Demming's forehead, and he crouched down instinctively to keep himself beneath its life-giving surface. "You are captain, yes?"

"Yes." Mendez also stooped down, keeping her head below the water though her long braid now floated on top.

"You keep your crew in line?"

It was an odd way to word the question, but she nodded. "Yes. They follow my orders." The water was now low enough that, even stooped, the back of her head and top of her shoulders were cresting the surface.

"Good." In one smooth, clearly practiced motion, Suwa Jem drew the strange pistol at his side. And fired.

Demming heard that same soft *whump* he'd heard before, only louder now.

Captain Mendez clutched at her chest and collapsed. She floated to the top of the water, but it was now at waist height and dropping rapidly.

"Captain!" Demming managed to gasp out, his voice sounding harsh and hoarse in the air that had replaced the ship's water. He reached out toward her, but the pirate captain swung his pistol in Demming's direction, and he froze.

The rest of the crew had all dropped to their knees, whether to stay underwater or from shock Demming couldn't tell, and he did the same, then let himself fall forward, face pressing against the cool, damp floor as the last of the water drained away, leaving only small, shallow pools and a few droplets.

Suwa Jem stomped over to stand above Demming, pistol

still trained on him. The pirate captain stared down at him, and Demming managed to lift his head, straining against the sudden weight of it, before collapsing again. The pirate snorted once, then holstered his pistol again and turned away. The other pirates followed his lead and marched out through the porthole. Demming could hear their odd triple footsteps clanging down the gangway, the sound echoing in the now-waterless ship. A distant hiss told him they had closed the door to engineering, and then he felt the *Remora* shake as the *Siren Knife* severed its door-seal and pushed off. Within seconds the sound and the tremor had faded, leaving the *Remora* cold, dry, and adrift.

Demming laid his head back down on the floor. He could see the captain's body not far away, but the effort of rising seemed too much. His eyes drifted shut.

# CHAPTER TEN

AFTER A FEW MINUTES—AT LEAST he thought they were minutes—Demming stirred. His gills rasped against his neck, his throat constricted, and his head began to feel light. Out of instinct his mouth dropped open and he took a deep, shuddering breath.

And started choking.

By the wave, that was awful! He always forgot how much harder it was to breathe air than water, and this air was stale and foul besides!

But as the air filled his lungs, he felt his head clear, and strength return to his limbs.

It was a good thing they were amphibious! And that the space pirates hadn't known that. Captain Mendez's plea had clearly convinced Suwa Jem that they could only breathe underwater, so the pirate captain had thought he was sentencing the entire crew to a quick death when he left. That had probably been the only thing preventing him from taking steps toward a more demonstrable death. The captain's ploy had saved them all.

All except her.

Demming's eyes flew open. Captain Mendez lay curled up on the floor not six feet from him. Her customary braid had come undone somehow, and long dark blond hair was splayed across her face and neck and shoulder. He didn't see any sign that she was breathing. Nonetheless, he pulled himself to his knees and crawled toward her.

"Captain?" No response. "Captain?" Now he was close enough to reach out and shake her by the shoulder. "Captain!"

Nothing. The shaking caused her body to shift, however, and she rolled partially onto her back, her head lolling to the side. The front of her uniform seemed charred and her skin was almost scalding, suggesting that the pirate pistol had produced some sort of heat. Most likely it had cooked her organs in an instant. Death would be equally fast, and painless after that first searing sensation. At least Demming hoped so.

The captain's eyes had scrunched shut after the shot, and they had not opened since. Demming was glad of that. At least he would not have to close her eyes the way he'd done for Holst.

But the end result was the same. Another member of the crew was dead. And they were without a captain.

And Jacobsen was in the crew quarters, farther down the ship.

He might be making his way in this direction already, but he was taking his time. Demming listened closely, and heard at least two people weeping and at least two more praying. The captain's death had struck them all hard. The crew might not know that Captain Mendez was dead, but everyone knew they'd just been captured and boarded, and by now they also knew the ship's entire water supply had been drained. Everyone was on edge. They were probably mere moments away from widespread panic.

Demming took a deep breath. He'd wanted to be Second Lieutenant, after all. That meant he had to handle matters in times like this, when the captain was incapacitated and the First Lieutenant was nowhere near the foredeck. Jacobsen could assume command later. Right now they just needed to keep everybody together and calm them down by distracting them with something else.

What else, he had no idea.

First things first. He used the captain's chair to pull himself to his feet. Then he walked over to where Amelia still lay, his leg muscles protesting from their long disuse. It felt so odd to have to lift each leg, and to feel his weight pushing him down against the floor, instead of floating and swimming so easily.

"Are you okay?" he asked the tall, slender engineer, crouching beside her. He reached out one hand and just barely brushed it against the bruise that stood out against her pale skin. "Did they hurt you beyond this?"

Amelia shook her head. "I'm—I'm okay," she managed to gasp out, pushing herself up to a sitting position. "He—he hit me, backhanded me, when I demanded to know what he wanted. And he—" she broke down, sobbing into her hands. Demming said nothing, just waited. "They killed Bixby!"

Bixby? He searched his memory. Ah, yes. Bixby Carruthers was one of Amelia's engineering crew. Decent enough fellow, though a bit of a temper. Short, stocky, fiery red hair. "He's dead?" That explained the whump and the thump he'd thought he'd heard earlier.

"He told them to unhand me," she explained quietly, rubbing at her eyes. "And the captain shot him! It was so awful!" The sobs threatened to return, and Demming knew he had to head them off somehow.

"What was the deal with those nets?" he asked quickly. "How did they steal our velocity, and did they damage the

*Remora* somehow or just steal whatever velocity she had at the time?" He took a deep breath, and something else occurred to him. "Mister Dittmers!"

The quartermaster had conveniently fallen back into his chair when he'd collapsed under the weight of the air. Now he glanced up, and after a second of searching his hangdog stare found Demming. "Yes, Mister Demming?"

"How are we breathing?" Demming asked him. He waved his hand around between them. "They stole our water—all of it. But they must have replaced it with air or we'd have suffocated. But why bother? They're space pirates, and clearly left us to die. Why give us air instead?

The heavyset quartermaster perked up slightly, the questions at least drawing his interest. "I have a theory as to the why of it," he admitted after a moment, rubbing his pudgy chin. "But as to how we're breathing at all"—he typed in a series of quick commands, and studied the results on-screen. "Looks like they flooded the *Remora* with a mix of oxygen, nitrogen, and carbon dioxide. Not all that different from the air back home."

Demming nodded. At least they wouldn't suffocate. "I definitely want to hear your theories about what just happened," he assured the other man. "Now may not be the best time, however. Right now we really need to know if they left us anything at all. And we need to let the others know that the air's fully breathable, too."

"I'll run a new inventory," the quartermaster promised, a gleam in his dark eyes. "And I'll notify Mister Jacobsen, Doctor Pyle, and Miss Scutt's second about the air." He concentrated on his screen, and began typing again.

Demming nodded and moved his gaze to the lone figure beyond the empty captain's chair. "Lizette, those nets stole all of our momentum," he pointed out, and the short, curvy pilot nodded. "Did they damage our engines, or just shut them down?"

As he'd hoped, asking after the *Remora*'s well-being—and her flight capability—snapped Lizette out of her shock, at least for now. "I'll see what I can do to get us underway again," she assured him, turning back to the wheel with the hint of a spark in her eye.

"I'd better get back to engineering and make sure they didn't create any additional havoc there as they left," Amelia pointed out, and though he'd rather have kept her on the foredeck with him Demming stood and offered her a hand up. He understood—right now she really needed to keep herself busy. So did everyone else.

Besides, the safety of everyone onboard probably depended upon getting the *Remora* moving again. And to do that, he needed Amelia running checks from below while Lizette worked on the problem from up here.

"Mister Pyle," he called out as Amelia staggered to the door and cycled it open. "I need you to check in with Mister Kesselman. Make sure everyone's all right in the crew quarters."

Pyle was already out of his seat. "Yes, sir!" The midshipman strode toward the door, his steps steady. Pyle was younger than all of the other officers save Craddick and possibly Molly Cuny, so he'd had land training more recently. Demming envied him that. It was going to take him several days to get used to this again. And it looked like he'd have that time, because unless they managed to find a large quantity of water somewhere out in the ether, the *Remora* was going to remain high and dry.

"Doctor Pasic?" he called out last, which was fine—all the others were now elsewhere or occupied.

"Mister Demming." Air was quieter than water, so it did far less to mask the sound of Dr. Pasic rising to his feet and making his way toward him.

"We'll need to make sure they didn't hurt anyone else," Demming pointed out as Pasic reached him. "But first—" he glanced over at Captain Mendez.

"Yes, well, there isn't much I can do in a situation like this," the tall, lean doctor explained as he sank down beside the captain. His long, slender hands moved quickly, checking for pulse and pupil dilation. After a moment he leaned back on his haunches and shook his head. "She's most definitely dead—without a full autopsy I can only guess, but I'd say death by some sort of internal convection. She was literally cooked in an instant." He sighed. "I can prepare her body for whatever funeral rites we choose to adopt, but that's about it."

"Let's do that, then," he told the doctor. "Get her ready as best you can." There wasn't any reason to wait, and the doctor's assignment would both get Captain Mendez off the foredeck and get her ready for burial.

That reminded Demming that they still needed to deal with Holst's body, and now with Bixby as well. And soon. It would probably best to take care of that in this atoll, while they were already at a standstill.

Pasic nodded and rose, heading for the door so he could retrieve the necessary tools and supplies from his office. Demming hoped the pirates had at least left them those. That took care of everyone on the foredeck. Which meant—he took a deep breath, then rose slowly and walked carefully back to his chair. Once there he dropped into it and thumbed the control for the sleeping-tube.

"Mister Jacobsen?" There was nothing but static on the

other end. "Mister Jacobsen, please report to the foredeck immediately. This is an emergency."

"On my way," the first lieutenant—about to become acting captain—replied after a minute. Demming relaxed slightly. Jacobsen was obviously still alive, which meant he didn't have to worry about assuming command himself. Jacobsen was far more comfortable ordering people around than he was, which was fine. In fact, right now they could all use a little more of that. In a crisis or a time of grief, it was always nice to have someone else tell you what to do.

That thought made Demming realize something, and he glanced around. Everyone on the foredeck now had an assignment of some sort.

Everyone except for him. What was he supposed to do while waiting for Jacobsen to take charge?

Demming pondered that for a minute. His job was to keep the officers and crew active, and he had done that. Soon Jacobsen would assume command. Lizette and Amelia would manage to get them moving again. Then they could continue sailing across the ether, returning to their original mission.

He glanced over to where Captain Mendez still lay, though at least Pasic had arranged her limbs in a more decorous sleeping pose. Poor Mendez. She'd been right not to resist, but it was frustrating and infuriating and very sad that taking that course of action had cost her her life.

Demming just hoped that would be the last of the *Remora*'s sacrifices.

# CHAPTER ELEVEN

THE STEADY THUMP OF FOOTSTEPS reached him a moment later, and Demming looked toward the door. One hand slid toward the knife in his boot, even though there was little chance any of the space pirates had remained—and if one had, his diving knife would never have penetrated their armor. Reaching for the weapon made him feel slightly better, however.

The approaching footsteps were the standard two-beat variety, though, and a moment later Jacobsen jogged into view. From the sweat on his brow it was clear that the short run from the crew's quarters had not been easy for him, and Demming vaguely remembered something about the other man's belittling surface exercises back during their cadet training. "No reason to ever go above water," Jacobsen had claimed, "and ridiculous to think we would ever have to breathe open air the way our first ancestors did."

He was probably regretting that position now.

"What happened?" Jacobsen demanded as he stepped heavily through the door and stopped, gasping for breath, to lean against the empty ensign's chairs. His dark curls were plastered to his forehead, and his eyes were wide in his dark face. Then he spotted the body on the floor, and he sank to his knees, skin pale.

"They killed the captain," Demming explained as calmly as he could. Seeing the usually cocky Jacobsen so undone was unnerving. "They also took all our water, and all our supplies." He reached down and offered the other man a hand up. "You're acting captain now."

For a moment his hand hung there, unnoticed, as Jacobsen stared at Mendez's body.

"Sir?"

No reply.

"Sir!"

At last Jacobsen looked up, though his eyes barely seemed to focus.

"You're acting captain now, sir," Demming told him again, deliberately making his tone brisk. "We need you to focus. Keep it together for the crew's sake, sir."

Jacobsen stared at him, then at his hand, then back up at him. Finally he nodded. "Yes, of course." He accepted Demming's grip and half rose, half let himself be hauled to his feet. "Of course." Then he straightened his rumpled jacket and stepped over to the command chair. "For the crew."

Demming followed as Jacobsen settled himself into the chair. The new acting captain sprang out of it again a moment later. "What is our status, Mister Demming?" he asked. There was still a hint of panic in his voice.

"Miss Mills and Miss Scutt are checking the engines and jets for damage," Demming explained, "and ascertaining how and when we can get underway again. Mister Dittmer is running a new inventory to discover whether the pirates left us anything usable, as well as formulating a theory on why they would pump breathable air into the *Remora* when they stole our water. Mister Pyle is coordinating with Mister Kesselman to make sure the crew are safe and remain calm, and Doctor Pasic is checking on any other injuries, and preparing both the captain and Mister Carruthers for burial at sea."

"Mister Carruthers?" Jacobsen blinked. Demming had never seen the other man look so lost.

"One of Miss Scutt's team," Demming supplied quietly. "They killed him when he tried to interfere."

"Ah." Jacobsen glanced around the foredeck, his eyes slowly registering the fact that only four of them were here— alive, at least—and the other two were keeping busy. He nodded. "Good work, Mister Demming," he admitted slowly, as if that recognition had cost him. "You've done an excellent job of focusing everyone on the tasks at hand."

"Thank you, sir." Demming waited, but Jacobsen had trailed off again and was staring out at the ether. "Space," the pirates had called it. The name certainly fit, but to Demming's mind "ether" was richer and more evocative.

"Convene a meeting of the officers as soon as feasible, please," Jacobsen stated suddenly. He sank back into the captain's chair. "We need to discuss everyone's findings and formulate a plan of action."

"Yes, sir." Demming started toward his own seat, then stopped. He shook his head and crossed behind the command chair, going to the First Lieutenant's chair instead. Now his chair. He'd never expected to be made first lieutenant, not of the *Remora*. And certainly not less than two weeks after their launch.

But then, no one could have expected what they would encounter out here.

Clearly, the royal scientists would have to reevaluate their understanding of the ether, and of their own world's role in that vastness.

Provided the *Remora* ever returned to share that knowledge with them.

Shrugging aside the morbid thought, Demming set about notifying the other officers of their new captain's first order. He made sure to include Mister Watkins, and to ask him to pull together any food he could. Even a token meal would help calm people's nerves, and Demming was sure the captain's weren't the only ones currently on edge.

"Thank you all for coming on such short notice," Jacobsen told them after everyone had gathered in the officers' mess. He'd spent the past hour staring out at the ether, but he seemed calmer now, and more in control. Some of his natural arrogance had returned, and though that brusque pride grated on Demming he was glad to see the acting captain coming out of his initial shock and taking charge. The ship couldn't afford to have its commanding officer foundering.

"This has been a difficult time," Jacobsen continued, pacing at the head of the table. His hands brushed the back of the captain's seat but he didn't pause, almost as if he still felt it would be improper for him to sit. Demming could hardly blame him for that. "We didn't even think there would be anyone else in the ether, much less pirates! And for them to attack us, and steal our supplies and our water, and kill the captain and Mister Carruthers—" Words failed him for a moment, and Demming watched quietly, holding his breath. Would Jacobsen break down again? Would he need to step up and take control? He hoped not.

After a moment Jacobsen recovered and continued. "I never expected to be captain here," he explained, "so I ask you to bear with me." Everyone nodded. No one blamed him for being overwhelmed by the change in his position. It would have been hard enough to have command thrust upon him suddenly, in any situation. But out here in the ether, in a ship they still had barely gotten used to, in a territory they still knew so little about? And with new enemies suddenly appearing out of nowhere and stripping them of their supplies? It would be enough to destroy anyone's confidence.

Fortunately, confidence was one thing Jacobsen had always had in abundance. "I understand everyone has been busy assessing damage and determining options," he continued, nodding at Demming but not otherwise acknowledging his efforts. Demming swallowed a burst of anger. Typical of Jacobsen not to give anyone else credit. Apparently the other man really was returning to form. "I think it would be best if we hear everyone's reports, and then I'll discuss our next move," the acting captain continued. "Miss Scutt, perhaps you had better start."

"Yes, sir." Pasic had obviously seen to her bruise, and except for a dark patch there on the cheek Amelia looked unfazed by the recent activities. Demming noticed that her hands shook slightly, however, and her voice wavered just a little as she spoke. "Fortunately, the pirates seemed to hold our technology in low regard. They inspected the *Remora* but sneered at her capabilities, and saw nothing worth taking in our engines or other systems. They didn't bother to damage anything, either—clearly they believed we were no threat to them, and would not be in a position to recover from their attack." Her hands clenched, and she wove her fingers together, her knuckles whitening as she squeezed to force herself calm. "The good news, then, is that we have taken no damage. Our hull is still intact, as are the scrubbers, the impellers, the maneuvering jets, and the rest."

Jacobsen nodded. "That is good news, thank you. What about getting underway again?"

Amelia glanced quickly at Demming. "The pirates removed their nets when they departed, so I didn't have an opportunity to study them directly, but it appears they used some kind of feedback circuit to siphon off our momentum, converting our kinetic energy to electrical and absorbing that. It's a clever system—the faster a ship is going, the more powerful the nets become. They didn't do any lasting damage, however. We should be able to fire up the impellers. We won't get a lot of speed from them, but it will be something."

Jacobsen nodded and shifted, his gaze settling on Lizette. It was clear he considered Amelia's report over, and Demming saw her frown slightly. He knew he was mirroring that expression. Was that it? That was all their new captain was planning to ask? He cleared his throat.

"Yes, Mister Demming?" For a second he saw the familiar glare rise in Jacobsen's gaze, but it quickly vanished. "Did you have something to add?"

"Yes, sir." Demming turned to look at Amelia. "Miss Scutt, what about the scrubbers? We're breathing air right now, and I'm assuming there is very little water left onboard"—he turned toward Dittmer, who nodded glumly—"which means we need to make the current atmosphere last. Can the scrubbers handle that?"

Amelia smiled at him gratefully. "They can, yes. Not in their current configuration—right now they're set up to draw the carbon dioxide out of the water, and we'll need to reset them a bit. It won't be difficult, though. I've studied plans for domed facilities in the air, and my team can make the necessary modifications. The air won't last forever—the process isn't perfect, and eventually the buildup of carbon dioxide will reach poisonous levels—but I'm certainly we can get at least two to three weeks out of our current atmosphere."

Demming nodded, and ignored the look of surprise and anger flickering across his captain's face as Jacobsen realized what a major question he'd overlooked. "Thank you, Miss Scutt. And what about our batteries? How does the ship stand on power?"

"Not good," she admitted. "Those nets drained us to ten percent of capacity. Once we get moving, however, we can recharge. Depending upon speed, we should be able to get back up to at least half strength in a few days."

"Thank you, Miss Scutt," Jacobsen cut in. He didn't even glance in Demming's direction, and Demming seethed. He also had a sinking feeling. Captain Mendez had always been more than willing to acknowledge any of her officers' contributions. He knew Holst would have done the same. But it was clear Jacobsen wouldn't work that way. He would try to take credit for any revelations and any smart decisions, would ignore others' involvement, and would probably foist blame for any mistakes off on his subordinates. Most notably the First Lieutenant who was already annoying him by pointing out his errors. This was not going to be easy.

"Miss Mills?" Jacobsen continued, turning toward the pilot. She nodded.

"Miss Scutt is right," Lizette replied, "there isn't any damage to our systems. We can get moving immediately. The impellers will only provide a weak amount of thrust, but the good news is out here in the ether that velocity will continue uninterrupted until we choose to brake or have to maneuver wildly." Her eyes glittered. "If we ever encounter nets like those again, I have some ideas on how to evade them, too—or turn them back on their owners." Demming smiled, as did a few of the others. Lizette was not a fan of coming in second, or of losing.

Jacobsen started to nod, but stopped when Demming caught his eye. "Sonic ram," Demming mouthed, and after a second his captain nodded.

"What about the sonic ram, Miss Mills?" Jacobsen asked, keeping his tone casual. "Would that be any help in increasing our velocity?"

Lizette blinked. "Yes, yes it would," she agreed, a smile curving her lips. "With these rocks all around us, we could push off from the nearest surface easily. Then we could trigger the impellers to add to that initial velocity. I think we could get at least a third of our former speed back by the time we exit this atoll." Her glance at Jacobsen carried new respect, and Demming pushed back the annoyance that caused him. The fact that Amelia gave him a warm, knowing smile helped considerably. As did Jacobsen's minute nod in his direction. If getting along with the new captain meant letting him take credit for an idea from time to time, so be it. That would be a small price to pay to keep the ship running smoothly.

"Mister Dittmer, how stand our supplies?" was Jacobsen's next question. "Did those pirates leave us anything at all?"

"They stripped the main holds clean, sir," Dittmer replied. But then a slow smile crept its way across his wide face. "But they were lazy, and in a hurry. They didn't touch any personal items, or inspect the other chambers thoroughly. We lost all of our backup supplies, and much of our food, and of course all of our water, but Doctor Pasic still has his full medical kit, engineering still has its tools and any equipment and materials stored in their own compartment, and we still have some basics like spare uniforms."

"They never even went near my galley," Watkins cut in, glancing apologetically at Dittmer. "So we've still got the food in there. I can stretch it out for a few weeks, no problem." He grinned quickly. "Though everyone may get a little sick of soup and crackers by the time we're done." That brought a brief ripple of much-needed laughter. Even Jacobsen cracked a smile.

Dittmer nodded affably, not at all put out by the cook's interruption, before continuing. "We also retained all of our personal weapons—the pirates never even searched for them." Demming remembered Captain Mendez telling the pirate captain that they didn't have any weapons onboard, and clenched his jaw. Her sacrifice had saved more than their lives, it seemed.

His shift drew Dittmer's eyes, and the quartermaster nodded in his direction. "I also have a theory as to why we have breathable air, sir."

Jacobsen stopped pacing and studied him. "Let's hear it."

"They pumped out all of our water," Dittmer explained. "Which means they had cargo holds sufficient to hold that much liquid. Those containers had to be pressurized to keep from exploding in the ether. The easiest way to maintain pressure is to fill the space with something else, something heavier than the ether to prevent it from slipping in." He grinned. "And the simplest, lightest thing to use is air." The grin vanished, leaving him serious. "We were extremely lucky, though. Clearly the pirates came from a world with air similar to our own, whether that is their own homeworld or simply their most recent stop. If they had been carrying pure nitrogen, or even pure oxygen, or some other element, we would have suffocated within minutes."

"Which is no doubt what they intended," Kesselman pointed out. Craddick was minding the crew, and Pyle the foredeck, so all the other officers could be present for this meeting. "Why give us something that would keep us alive?"

"They didn't mean to," Pasic agreed. The doctor looked as grim as Demming had ever seen him. "The captain made a point of begging them not to take the water, and stressed that we needed it to survive. They had no reason to suspect we could breathe air as well. They fully intended to leave us dead behind them."

That brought a moment's silence as everyone grasped how narrowly they'd escaped death, and how their captain had bought them that reprieve.

After a minute, Jacobsen frowned and pushed his chair aside, leaning forward and setting both hands flat on the desk.

"I have reached a decision," he announced, and something in his tone put Demming instantly on alert. There was a guardedness there, and a hint of subdued panic, that told him the acting captain was about to do something foolish.

"We have suffered a major loss," Jacobsen continued, "not just in personnel but in supplies. We have enough air for a few weeks, and another food as well. And we still have no idea how far it might be to our original destination. I think it's safe to say, however, that the light's source is considerably farther than a few weeks' away, even at full speed."

He paused to glance at Lizette, who nodded after a moment. There was no way to be certain what their top speed was out here, of course, but Demming guessed she was using their previous velocity as a gauge.

"Given that," Jacobsen went on, "I have decided. There is no way we can continue this mission with any hope of success.

Instead, we will be turning back toward home."

There was an instant uproar throughout the mess, and several officers leaped to their feet, protests loud on their lips as they turned to argue against the acting captain's decision.

Demming was almost surprised to realize he was among them.

# CHAPTER TWELVE

"TURN BACK? WE CAN'T!" DEMMING shouted. Nor was he the only one. Amelia, Lizette, and Quentin were on their feet as well. Dittmer and Kesselman looked surprised but didn't leave their seats or open their mouths. Pasic's face bore no expression whatsoever.

Jacobsen looked surprised by the force of his subordinates' objection, but then his jaw tightened and his brow sank. Uh-oh. "Of course we can," he replied, his voice already several octaves lower than before, "and we will. That is all."

"No, that isn't all," Demming and the others argued. "We don't know how far away we are at this point," Lizette pointed out, "or how long it will take to get back, or even exactly what course to set."

"We don't know how the effect a return once we get there, even if we do turn back," Amelia added.

"We haven't completed our mission," Demming said simply. Quentin nodded, as did the other two, but it was him the captain glared at.

"Completing the mission is no longer an option," Jacobsen told him bluntly. "We don't have the supplies, the speed, or even the air, let alone the water, to make it the rest of the way—

and that's assuming we knew how far we had to go in the first place!" His voice rose dangerously on the last words, and sweat stood out on his brow. "This was supposed to be a simple exploratory mission! Instead we've got two dead officers and one dead crewman! There are pirates out here, and probably others we don't know about as well! And we're not equipped to deal with any of them!" Jacobsen's words were spilling out of him now. "We need to go home, while we still can!"

It was clear their acting captain was losing it. Demming forced himself to calm down and keep his voice level. Getting upset right now would only make matters worse. "All right," he agreed, spreading his hands in front of him. Jacobsen started at the motion anyway. "All right, maybe we do need to go back. At least for supplies, if nothing else. Perhaps we could find some way to stop just outside the air barrier and the Navy could launch a small probe toward us, carrying water and food and heavier weapons. Then we could resume our mission fully stocked and better equipped." Several of the others nodded. "But we don't need to turn back just now, do we?" He turned toward Lizette and Amelia. "Do you think, with the rocks here to bounce off from, we could build up to the same speed we had before?"

Both ladies nodded cautiously. "I'd need to do some calculations," Amelia admitted, "but I think we could, yes."

"Okay. And we have a few weeks of air at this point, is that right?" She nodded. "And a few weeks of food?" Both Quentin and Dittmer confirmed that. "Then we could continue toward the light source for a few more days, a week at most. Get past this atoll, see what else is out there, gather more data. Then we could turn around and head home. That would leave us enough time to get back before our food and air ran out. And we'd have more information than we would otherwise. Every day we're out here, we learn something new, something no one back home has even imagined. Think about how much more we could find out with just a few more days' travel!"

Everyone in the room was nodded and muttering their agreement, and Demming felt a burst of pleasure and pride. He thought he'd made an excellent argument, and it was clear his fellow officers felt the same.

All except the one who mattered.

Jacobsen was now scowling at him full-force, and Demming remembered with a lurch how angry the other man got whenever anyone dared to question his opinion. He'd even raised his voice at Captain Mendez once or twice, though she had shut that down in short order. Now he was the captain, and he didn't have to put up with arguments from anyone.

Especially the man he knew had been gunning for the same position on the *Remora*, and who was now his second-in-command.

"I see your point, Mister Demming," Jacobsen replied sharply, emphasizing Demming's lower rank. "And they are valid ones. But the safety of this ship and her crew are paramount. I cannot guarantee that safety if we proceed. Therefore, we are turning back. Now."

"We won't be any safer if we turn back," Demming pointed out quickly, realizing only after he'd opened his mouth that he should have let someone else make that observation. Still, Jacobsen was already pissed with him. No point dragging anyone else into the captain's ire. "We don't know what else is between us and home, either. Going forward for a few more days won't really put us at any further risk, and we'll learn more in the process." And get a little closer to our original goal, he thought but chose not to mention.

"We have already passed through the ether that separates us from home," the captain countered, stepping toward Demming and stopping when only a few paces separated them. The fact that Demming was a few inches taller probably didn't help matters any. "For all we know, we are on the very edge of pirate waters, as it were, and going further would subject us to constant attack. We might not survive a second such encounter."

This close, Demming could see the fear in the captain's eyes, and suddenly he understood. This wasn't about the safety of the ship and her crew. It was about Jacobsen's safety. He was terrified. Mendez had sacrificed herself to save the rest of them from the *Siren Knife* and her crew. Jacobsen was afraid another run-in with pirates would require him to make a similar gesture. And he wasn't man enough to do it.

Demming felt a wave of pity for the other man. For all his bluster, Jacobsen was just scared. He wasn't even a coward, necessarily. Anyone would be frightened by the thought of having to die to save others. The brave did it anyway, if it became necessary. But not being brave didn't make you a coward. It made you normal.

Unfortunately, Jacobsen wasn't about to admit to that failing. He was a proud man, too proud, and he'd always held himself as better than everyone around him. To recognize his own fear was a terrible blow.

And like a wounded shark, he was at his most dangerous when he was injured.

To make matters worse, Demming saw the captain's eyes widen slightly and then narrow, and knew with a jolt that his own gaze had betrayed his thoughts. And his pity. And if there was one thing that could drive a man like Jacobsen to rage, it was another's pity.

"Did you wish to argue the point, Mister Demming?" Jacobsen's voice was a mere hiss now, the words sliding from between clenched teeth. "Or are you prepared to accept your captain's orders, as befits a true officer?"

The words stung, just as intended. And as Jacobsen had also no doubt intended, Demming finally lost his own temper. "I fully intend to behave as befits a true officer, sir," he snapped, leaning in slightly to look down upon his nominal superior. "Which means obeying the directives we were given before launch, and following through with our mission as ordered. Sir."

The captain turned away with a smirk. "I can see you will insist upon being unreasonable, Mister Demming," he commented, walking back behind his chair and leaning on it to reinforce his authority. "You are a stubborn man, and it is clear you have set your mind on this foolhardy course. Very well." He flashed a quick, razor grin. "You are hereby confined to the brig until such time as I see fit to release you. Mister Kesselman, please see to it that he gets there safely and without delay." And Jacobsen shifted to gaze down the table, dismissing Demming from consideration and view at the same time.

The sentence brought fresh shouts from several of the other officers, even as Kesselman rose slowly to his feet. But Jacobsen glowered at each and every one in the room in turn, and the threat evident in his gaze shut down further protest.

"You're letting your own fear get in the way of your duty," Demming told him as the bo'sun approached. "Don't. We have a job to do, and the High Command and the Queen expect us to do it. There are risks, yes, but we knew that was a possibility when we volunteered. Don't throw away our mission, and the sacrifices of Captain Mendez, Mister Holst, and Mister Carruthers, just because you're scared for your own skin."

Jacobsen bristled visibly, lips pulling back from his teeth in a fierce scowl, and he looked ready to leap upon Demming then and there. But Kesselman stepped between them, his back to the captain, and effectively ended that confrontation. "Will you walk with me, sir?" he asked quietly.

For half a second Demming considered resisting. Kesselman was bigger, heavier, and stronger, but he was faster. He might be able to get past the bo'sun. But then what? Jacobsen was no pushover—he was strong too, and fast, and right now he was spoiling for a fight. Besides, if Demming did resist he would face far worse charges than stubbornness and potential insubordination. And Jacobsen would have every right to turn the rest of the crew upon him. Far better to cooperate for now, and retain the sympathy of the others. So he nodded. "Of course, Mister Kesselman."

Kesselman indicated the door, and Demming walked toward it, the bo'sun right behind him. He tapped the panel and stepped through as soon as the porthole had irised open, leaving the chamber and the fight without a backward glance.

This was not over, however.

No, he had a feeling it was just beginning.

# CHAPTER THIRTEEN

WHEN HE'D FIRST SEEN THE designs for the *Remora*, Demming had laughed. "A brig?" he'd asked the instructor. "Really? Who exactly are we going to toss in there—the etheric equivalent of sea snails? Maybe an eel or two?"

"Brigs are for more than captives," the instructor, a ramrod-straight older woman with steely hair and an equally stern countenance, had warned. "Sometimes they're for crew as well."

That was certainly true, but he hadn't seen how one could possibly be necessary here. Every member of the crew would be doubly a volunteer—they'd all chosen to join the Royal Navy, and then they'd each chosen to try for a berth on the ethership. Brigs were from troublemakers and shirkers and mutineers. Why would any of those types ever bother to try for a place on the *Remora*?

He'd never suspected he'd be the first to put the brig to use. Or that he'd be the one held there, rather than the one locking someone else up.

"I'm really sorry about this, sir," Kesselman told him quietly as they trudged down the gangway. The offiers' mess was in the midsection near the foredeck, so that they could get to and from the command cabin in a hurry if necessary. The brig was set near the front, by the crew quarters, so that anyone captive there would be close enough for the sailors to check on regularly. The distance seemed even further now that they had to walk it instead of swimming it.

"I know," Demming assured him. He could see the bo'sun's reluctance in his gait, and his expression, which was even more downcast than usual. "You're just following orders."

"I'm sure he'll cool off soon," Kesselman offered slowly. "He's just a little wound up, is all. What with everything that's happened."

"We all are, Mister Kesselman," Demming pointed out, but softly. "We all are." He didn't bother to add that Jacobsen was the only one acting irrationally as a result. There was no point getting into that, and especially not with the boatswain. Kesselman was good at following orders. That's why Jacobsen had chosen him to escort Demming to the brig. That and his sheer size, which made it less likely Demming would try anything.

They walked in silence the rest of the way. Finally they reached the porthole, which unlike every other entry on the ship required both a code and the manual doorwheel. Demming waited quietly as Kesselman punched in the code and spun the wheel, pulling the heavy door open. If he'd wanted to run, that would have been the time, with the bo'sun occupied and no one else in sight. But it's not like there was anywhere to go. Besides, he didn't want to get Kesselman in trouble.

The door slid outward to reveal a decent-sized compartment, roughly four times the size of an officer's quarters. Bunks were mounted in the wall on both sides and across the far wall, and a privy stood behind a small built-in screen. There was nothing else in the brig—no tables, no chairs, no windows. No bars, either, but that's because they didn't need any. The heavy door only opened from the outside, and that was security enough.

"Can I bring you a book or a deck of cards, sir?" Kesselman offered. "The captain didn't say you weren't allowed."

"No, thank you." Demming smiled to let the bo'sun know there were no hard feelings. "Maybe later. For now I think I'll just stretch out, catch up on my sleep." He winked. "You never know, this might turn out to be a blessing in disguise—as long as I'm in here, I can't be on the duty roster."

Kesselman chuckled with him. "Well, I'll leave you to it, then." He saluted. "I'm sure this'll pass soon, sir."

"I hope so," Demming muttered as he watched the bo'sun step back and swing the door shut behind him. It clanged shut with a heavy finality. "I certainly hope so." But I'm not counting on it, he thought as he sat on one of the bunks and swung his legs up. He had a feeling he might be here for a while.

He must have fallen asleep, because the thump of the doorwheel cycling open woke him. Groggily he sat up, glancing around. No way to tell how much time had passed, but from the fuzziness in his head it must have been hours, at least. Was it dinner time? Was that why Kesselman had returned? Or had the bo'sun been right, and Jacobsen had only needed time to cool down? Demming set his feet on the floor and rose, a little wobbly as he tried to make himself presentable again.

The door swiveled away to reveal a figure standing before it. But it wasn't Kesselman. Tall and lithe, long braid swaying behind her, Demming felt his head clear as he blinked to confirm what he was seeing.

"Amelia?"

Then another figure stepped up beside her, as tall but far

broader, almost brutish. Demming knew without having to squint that this one's head would gleam as if bald in the gangway's light, despite its full head of fine, pale hair. Kesselman.

He'd expected the boatswain, of course. But why was Amelia here? Unless this was just a friendly visit. Somehow, though, he didn't think Jacobsen would allow him such a luxury.

Nor was he wrong. Once the door was open Amelia stepped over the sill. But Kesselman did not join her. Instead he heaved the door shut again. A moment later Demming heard it grind closed and locked once more.

"Cozy little place," Amelia remarked, glancing around. "Love what you've done with it." Her lips quirked into a small smile. "Hope you don't mind sharing."

"I welcome the company," Demming told her gallantly, which was certainly true. If he had to be cooped up with anyone, he'd rather it was her. But still—"What are you doing here, though?"

"Locked in, same as you," she answered, perching on the bunk next to the one he'd taken. "I was being 'insubordinate and obstinate.'"

Demming moved over to sit beside her, though he was careful not to crowd her. "What happened?"

"I told him he was a fool, and likely to kill us all!" she snapped, then sighed. "Sorry. You're not the one I'm angry at. If anything, you're the only one who's stood up to him."

"And look what I've earned for my troubles," Demming reminded her, gesturing around them. "What has he done now?"

"He's still dead-set on taking the *Remora* home," Amelia explained, leaning back against the bulkhead. She twisted her braid down over her shoulder and tugged absently at the end as she spoke. "Lizette and I confimed that we could probably come close to matching our previous speed—your idea about the sonic ram was brilliant." She smiled at his raised eyebrow. "Yes, I saw you mouth it at him. And I know he wouldn't have thought of it on his own." Then she turned serious again. "He wants us underway immediately, as soon as we've reconfigured the scrubbers and locked in our return course. Won't be more than a few hours from now."

Demming frowned. "I'm not happy about turning tail, either," he admitted, leaning back as well and lacing his hands together around one knee, "but if we're forced to return home, so be it. I don't see how that's putting our lives at risk."

"Because he doesn't want to stop at reaching our world," Amelia answered. "He wants to get back under the waves as soon as possible. No matter what."

"He's scared," Demming said quietly, remembering the look he'd seen in the acting captain's eyes. "Terrified, actually. He doesn't want to die out here."

Amelia surprised him by snorting. "None of us do! Even Lizette and Molly don't have a death-wish, for all that the one's obsessed with going fast and the other loves to shoot things. We all want to live long, healthy, happy lives. But his fear is making him irrational." She took a deep breath, visibly forcing herself to calm down. "I warned him that we might not be able to take the *Remora* back into the air, not without endangering her and ourselves."

This was news to Demming, and he twisted to study her. "Why not?"

"It's the velocity," she explained. "Even if we brake hard as we can right before we reach our world, we're going to need some speed to pierce that barrier we went through before. You remember how bumpy that was. Well, it'll be even worse heading in, because gravity will be pulling us down. We'll also be going from low pressure to higher pressure, but without the luxury of slowly depressurizing. We'll be lucky if all we get is a severe case of the bends."

The thought made Demming shudder. He'd had the bends—everyone experienced them at some point growing up, but during officer training they forced cadets to go through it again, in order to learn how to function through the pain. It wasn't an experience he was eager to repeat.

"What's the solution, then?" he asked.

"Well, we can do what you suggested," Amelia told him. "Do a full stop right before hitting that barrier, ferry supplies up or people down. A smaller ship could rise just high enough to reach us, then fall back, taking a portion of the crew along. That would take longer than the *Remora* descending, but it'd be a lot safer." She frowned. "The other option is to bring the *Remora* in, but carefully. Stop just outside again, then give her just enough momentum to pierce that barrier. Once she's in air she'll fall toward the water all on her own, and if she's pointed prow downward she should pierce it cleanly." That "should" worried him. "There's no way to be certain, of course. I don't think the royal scientists really thought about our return enough." She grinned quickly. "They just wanted us up and away as soon as possible."

Demming laughed. "So did we," he pointed out. He thought about what she'd just told him. "All right, so we have some options for when we get back."

"Yes, but Jacobsen refuses to consider them." Amelia twisted her braid around her fingers and tugged on it, scowling.

"He's ordering Lizette to set a course straight back to the Navy Shipyards, and use whatever speed she can muster to berth the *Remora* there as soon as possible." She shuddered. "If Lizette doesn't slow down enough, we might not survive the pounding we'll take when we hit the air. And even if we do, she'll just ram us into the shipyards like a harpoon imbedding itself in a whale!"

Demming rose to his feet—he still wasn't used to doing that in air, and it took him a second of floundering to remember how much effort was required to lever himself off the bench without flinging himself across the room or, worse, onto the floor. "So you told him all this, and he threw you in here?" He started pacing the floor.

"Yes. Told me I wasn't willing to obey orders, so I needed to be relieved of my duties." She almost growled. "I could have decked him!" That startled Demming, and told him just how upset she really was. Except in combat training, he'd never seen Amelia throw a single aggressive move at anyone. And even there she'd been a bit hesitant about it.

"This is bad," Demming stated as he walked. "He's lost his mind."

"Absolutely," she agreed.

"He's putting everyone in jeopardy, all because he's frightened."

"Yes."

"We need to stop him." He halted and turned to her. "We have to stop him."

"How?" She sat up, and they faced each other, only a few feet apart.

He couldn't believe he was about to say this. "We have to remove him from command. He is not in a clear state of mind."

"You're talking mutiny."

"Yes." He nodded slowly, then more firmly as he made up his mind. "Yes, I suppose I am."

Amelia smiled at him, the sight warming him like the rays of the morning sun.

"What do we do first?"

# CHAPTER FOURTEEN

"WE NEED SOMEONE TO LET us out." Demming decided. He clenched one hand in a fist and pounded into his other palm. "That's the first step. We can't do anything while we're trapped in here."

For half a second he thought he saw a glimmer of something in his companion's pretty eyes. Something—teasing? Flirtatious? Hungry? Then it was gone, and he wondered if he'd imagined it.

"Kesselman will never let us out," she said, any trace of other thoughts completely obscured. "That's why he's the perfect guard. I know he doesn't particularly agree with Jacobsen—at least, not about locking us up—but he's loyal to a fault." She looked down at her hands. "And not bright enough to worry about much beyond following orders."

Demming could tell she felt guilty about that assessment, but it was no worse than his own, and completely accurate. Kesselman wasn't the key.

But then who was?

"Jacobsen doesn't trust me, and right now he won't trust you either," he pointed out. "There's no way we'll get him to visit us in here, and he won't allow Lizette or Quentin either.

He knows they're on our side." It seemed ridiculous, and more than a little inappropriate, to be discussing sides on a ship. But there it was. If they were really going to overhrow the current captain, they had to divide the crew into their side and his side.

And if they guessed wrong, they'd be in far worse trouble than simply tossed in the brig. Mutiny was still a hanging offense.

"Molly's probably with us," Amelia said slowly, and Demming noticed that she hadn't even tried to argue the question of sides. He nodded. She might be righ—Molly Cuny was hard to read, and kept to herself, but she'd been excited about the *Remora*'s mission. And he knew she also hungered for payback against the *Siren Knife*. As did he. If they turned tail and headed for home, she'd never get the chance to even the score with that pirate ship. That wouldn't sit well with her.

"I doubt Jacobsen would let her visit us, though," he said, pacing again. "And how would we convince her to? You know how solitary she is."

"He might let Dittmer in to see us," Demming mused aloud, thinking as he walked back and forth. "But I don't know for certain that we could sway him to help us. You know how he is—we're less people than one more line in his inventory, and I don't think replacing an item sits well with him."

Then he brightened. "Got it! I know the one person Jacobsen has to let see us—if we can only convince him that we need him, and then to help us." Amelia stared at him, her hands stilling where they'd been clutching at her braid again. "Who?"

So he told her.

And she smiled. "Well, getting him down here is the easy part. Just do what I say."

~ * ~

An hour or so later—he still had a hard time telling time in here—Demming heard someone at the door. Was it another prisoner, captive of Jacobsen's paranoid tyranny? Or was it a meal?

The sight of Kesselman and a crewman answered that question. The crewman held two trays. Clearly Jacobsen felt that, since they were heading back now, he didn't need to ration the food.

Kesselman gestured for the crewman to precede him through the door, but stopped once he was inside and saw Amelia stretched out on the floor and Demming kneeling over her. "What happened?"

"I don't know," Demming replied, trying to project fear and concern in his voice. "We were just talking and she—she stopped, sniffed, wrinkled her nose, muttered something about the scrubbers. Then she collapsed! I've been trying to wake her, but she's not responding!"

Kesselman gestured for the crewman to set the trays down on one of the bunks—one of the far bunks, Demming noted, which would prevent him from grabbing them and using them as weapons—and crouched on Amelia's other side. Out of his reach. The bo'sun might not be the brightest of men, but he was smart enough not to allow a prisoner—even a wrongly imprisoned one—any opportunity. He placed a hand on Amelia's forehead, then pulled it back. "She's cold and clammy!"

"I know!" Demming leaned back on his heels and wrung his hands. "I'm really worried!" He hoped he wasn't overdoing it.

"I'll get the doctor." Kesselman scrambled awkwardly to his feet. "Don't worry. I'll have him here in a jiffy."

He turned hastily toward the door, only belatedly

remembering to gesture for the waiting crewman to accompany him. The two of them exited hurriedly, and the door slid shut again.

As soon as it was locked, Amelia opened her eyes and propped herself up on her elbows.

" 'I'm really worried?'" She echoed, grinning. "That's the best you can do? If I'd really fainted, is that all I'd get, that you were really worried?"

There was an undercurrent of something more serious behind her teasing, and Demming responded with the truth instead of a retort. "No, I'd probably be too concerned and upset to speak properly," he admitted quietly. "But I didn't think that would play well."

She studied him for a moment, gazing into his eyes, her lips ever so slightly parted. Under other circumstances, Demming might have taken that as an invitation to kiss her. But this was neither the time nor the place, and he wasn't entirely sure it was an invitation of that sort, so he restrained himself. With considerable effort.

"Probably not," she agreed finally, glancing away, a blush rising to her pale cheeks. "But thank you." She sat up fully. "You were right, though. So now we wait, and hope he sends Pasic in alone?"

Demming nodded. "I think he will. It's tactically smarter to lock the doctor in with us, and only open the door again once Pasic's signaled he's done. Otherwise he's got to keep the door open, and that's not secure. Or put a crewman in with us, but whoever it is won't dare say anything if Pasic orders him not to."

"Do you really think we can convince him?"

"I hope so." Demming remembered the doctor's completely

blank expression back in the officers' mess. "We have to." He changed the subject. "That trick with your forehead really worked."

Amelia laughed. "I know—my sisters and I used to do it all the time when we were kids and didn't want to go to school. Fooled them every time." She confounded Demmig when she'd licked her hand and then rubbed it across her forehead, but it had certainly produced the right effect.

Now he just hoped they could convince Pasic as easily as they'd fooled Kesselman.

It was only a few minutes later that they heard footsteps approach once more. Amelia quickly lay back down, eyes shut, limbs in roughly the same position as before. Demming, who had risen to his feet to stretch and restore circulation, lowered himself to his knees again. They were both back in their places as patient and worried companion when the door cycled open. Demming glanced back and was relieved to see Pasic standing there, med-kit in hand.

"What happened?" the doctor demanded at once, stepping quickly into the brig and hurrying to Amelia's side. Unlike Kesselman he didn't worry about placement or security, and dropped down right beside Demming to feel Amelia's forehead and then check her pulse. Which was rapid due to her getting up and jogging in place for a few minutes.

Demming repeated his story about her fainting, then glanced back at Kesselman. The bo'sun stood in the open door, clearly worried as well. Demming felt a little bad about tricking the man. Kesselman was a good sort.

Unfortunately, his presence meant Demming and Amelia couldn't drop their charade and talk to the doctor plainly.

Which was why he glanced back very deliberately now. The bo'sun nodded to him, then stiffened slightly as he realized the opening his presence presented. He quickly stepped back and swung the door shut, and the whir of the doorwheel filled the brig.

"I don't see—" Pasic was saying, when Amelia's eyes flew open.

"Wait," she pleaded, raising a hand to his arm as he started to rise to his feet. "Please. Hear us out."

Pasic was no fool—his eyes narrowed as he glanced from her to Demming and back. "This was all a trick. You aren't in any distress at all." But at least he made no move to leave.

"We are, actually," Demming corrected. "We're distressed about what's happening. Aren't you? Jacobsen's clearly taken leave of his senses. He'll kill us all, just because he's worried about sharing Captain Mendez's fate."

He and Amelia watched Pasic carefully, holding their breaths. This was the moment that mattered. If the doctor dismissed their concerns, they were lost. Oh, they could try to overpower him, but that wouldn't convince Kesselman to release them. They'd have a captive, but they'd still be imprisoned themselves, and Jacobsen would continue his mad plan unopposed.

Demming almost shouted when, after a long pause, the doctor nodded his head once. "I concur. He is behaving irrationally. I heard Miss Scutt's explanation of what could happen if we attempted to re-enter the air of our world, and saw him dismiss those arguments without consideration." He frowned. "But what is it you hope to accomplish by luring me in here?"

Amelia snorted. "Please. You're not stupid—far from it. You know exactly what we're doing."

That got a tight smile from the tall, lean doctor. "Yes, I suppose I do. You want me to call to Mister Kesselman, tell him I'm finished, and get him to open the door. Then you can presumably overpower him, make for the foredeck, and try to wrest control from our acting captain."

"That's pretty much it in a conch shell," Demming agreed. "Lizette will side with us. I think Pyle will as well, if he's present." He knew the young midshipman looked up to him, and hated the fact that he was willing to abuse that admiration, even if it was in a noble cause. "I don't know about Dittmer. Even if he doesn't, though, that's three to two, at worst. If we can subdue Jacobsen, the others will give over at once. I don't think any of them fully support his plan, it's just that Dittmer and Kesselman will obey him because he's acting captain."

Pasic nodded. He rummaged through the med-kit, then withdrew a small syringe and an ampule. Demming and Amelia both watched silently as the doctor filled the syringe and tested it. They both started when he squirted a tiny spray of the liquid out into the air.

"This will render our good boatswain unconscious," Pasic explained finally, rising to his feet and moving the syringe behind his back. "That way he will not be responsible for our actions, or forced to choose sides. If you would, please resume your tableau."

Demming hid a smile as Amelia flopped back down on the floor and closed her eyes yet again. It seemed they'd won an active co-conspirator rather than a grudging accomplice.

Behind him, Pasic pounded on the door. "Mister Kesselman!" A second later they heard the lock glide open, followed by the door itself.

"I'm done here, for now," the doctor announced as he

stepped through the door. "I'll check on her again in an hour or so."

"Is she gonna be all right," Kesselman asked, leaning in to peer at Amelia.

Which is when Pasic stuck him in the back of the neck with the syringe.

"She will be fine, Mister Kesselman," the doctor assured, removing the now-empty syringe and nodding at Demming to join him. "As will you, after your brief nap."

The bo'sun turned toward him, confusion and surprise dawning on his broad face, followed by anger, but that last was quickly washed away by unconsciousness.

Demming barely managed to get there in time to catch the bulky boatswain before he hit the ground.

With Pasic's help he maneuvered Kesselman over to one of the side bunks and lay him down. Then they returned to the door. Amelia had already stepped through, and nodded. The gangway was clear. Apparently Kesselman had not seen a need to bring a crewman with him this time.

"Very well, Mister Demming," Pasic commented as they swung the heavy brig door shut and spun the wheel, sealing the poor bo'sun inside. "Lead on. This is your mutiny, after all."

Demming grinned in reply, and even got a small smile in return. Amelia gave him a broader one, though the expression was a bit grimmer than her usual rare beams.

Together, the three of them set forth for the foredeck, and the captain they hoped to overthrow.

# CHAPTER FIFTEEN

"DO YOU HAVE A PLAN?" Pasic asked as they neared the foredeck. They'd been lucky enough to make it past the crew quarters without anyone seeing them—Demming was sure Jacobsen had broadcast the news of his incarceration, in the hopes of turning everyone against him.

"Not really," he admitted. "Planning isn't exactly my strong suit."

"Now he tells us," Amelia muttered behind him, but when he threw a glance her way she grinned. She actually seemed to be enjoying all this. She'd always struck him as a little on the reserved side, but ever since launch she'd been more active, more outgoing, more talkative. More flirtatious.

He certainly wasn't objecting.

"We could simply overpower him," Demming pointed out. "Unless Dittmer and Kesselman are both there, and Lizette and Pyle aren't, we should outnumber him."

The doctor frowned. "A bit too genuinely mutinous for my taste," he admitted. "And it's the kind of thing that can cause bad blood among the crew—even if you won, you might have several of the others angry at you for your actions, and that'll create more friction, rather than less."

"I'm not worried about friction so much as staying alive," Demming admitted under his breath. If the others heard they didn't respond.

"We could try to convince him that stepping down is in everyone's best interest," Amelia offered. The slender engineer glanced down at her hands rather than meet both Demming and Pasic's stunned looks. "All right, it was only a thought."

"If he was willing to listen to reason, we could have swayed him in the first place," Demming pointed out. "Instead of being thrown in the brig." He scratched at his cheek. "I could try to prove him unfit for duty, and relieve him that way."

That earned a snort from the doctor. "That sort of thing never actually works," he warned. "As long as Jacobsen's cool enough to retain control, he's sane enough to be in control. And he won't fall for you egging him on. Why should he? All you have to throw at him are empty words, and words aren't what he's afraid of."

Demming stopped and stared at the taller man. "You're right," he agreed slowly, as an idea began to form. A crazy idea. A ridiculous idea. A horribly inappropriate idea. But one that just might work. "It's not words that he's afraid of. But I know what is."

Then he turned and led them, not to the foredeck, but away from it. Toward the gunnery.

As he'd expected, Molly Cuny was in the cramped little cabin. Demming and others had long suspected she slept here, curled up among the weapons consoles and targeting arrays and racks of harpoon heads and net canisters.

When he stepped into the room, she glanced at him. Was that a small smile on her lips? It was hard to tell beneath the mass of curls. She sounded amused, though, when she said, "This isn't exactly the brig."

"Oh, good, I thought we'd made a wrong turn," he replied, which earned at least a headshake and a toss of hair. "Listen, Molly, we need your help." Amelia and Pasic had followed him in, and Pasic cycled the door shut behind him. The room was barely big enough to accommodate the four of them without bumping elbows or toes.

"I could pack you into a net canister and fire you into the ether," the tiny little gunner's mate mused, her fingers gliding across the net-launcher controls. As always when she talked about weapons or shooting things, her voice was louder, clearer, and much sharper. "Given what she said"—she flicked a finger in Amelia's direction—"you should be able to keep going indefinitely. No water or air, of course, but how long can you hold your breath?"

He was mostly certain she was kidding.

"Not exactly the kind of help we were looking for," he admitted, leaning back against one of the racks. "We need to do something about Jacobsen. Before he gets us all killed."

"The hand weapons are over there," Molly replied, waving at a rack toward the far corner. "Help yourselves."

"We don't want to hurt anybody," Amelia told her, and the smaller woman managed to look both disappointed and unconcerned at the same time. "We just want—what exactly do we want, Nate?"

"We want you to pretend the *Siren Knife* is back." Demming watched all three sets of eyes stare at him in shock and horror. "We can contact Lizette from here, fill her in via her own console so Jacobsen won't overhear, get her to play along. Between the two of you, we should be able to fake the pirate ship's return."

"You'll drive the whole ship into a mad panic," Pasic pointed out quietly. He said each word slowly, as if he were speaking to an inattentive child. "I know we want to deal with him, but surely there's some other way?"

"Maybe, but I can't think of one right now," Demming told him. He shrugged. "Look, we're only talking about the foredeck. Nobody else even needs to hear about this. So that's, what, five people, maybe? And one of them will be in on it." He rubbed the top of his head. "Yes, I know it's a terrible thing to do to any of them. And we can't tell the others what we're up to, or Jacobsen will never believe it's real. We have to trick them, too. And I'll feel bad about that. But if it gets Jacobsen to step down . . ."

Amelia was tugging at her braid, eyes far away. "I'll need to speak with Xander," she said finally. "You can't pull this off with engineering. You have to fake the ship linking to us, after all."

"You're right." Demming sighed. "And Jacobsen will warn the crew what's going on, same as Mendez did. So we either need a way to stop Kesselman from rousing the sailors or a way to get him to give us some space—or a way to deal with all of them."

To his surprise, Pasic smiled. "I believe I can be of assistance there." Then he laughed. Laughed! Demming wasn't sure what to make of this new side to the usually aloof doctor. "All Royal Navy ships are equipped with medical quarantine measures," Pasic explained. "In the event of a viral infection or some other widespread ailment, the ship's doctor has the authority to lock down various cabins and corridors."

"You can lock the crew in their quarters?" Demming stared at him. "Remind me never to piss you off."

"It's a grave misuse of my authority," the doctor replied, raising his chin, "and one that could easily have me stripped of my commission. If we weren't to succeed." He smirked a little. "But I fully expect your ad hoc little plan to work, so I'm not terribly worried."

"All right, so that's the crew taken care of," Demming agreed. He wanted to stand and pace—he did his best thinking while moving—but the gunnery was simply too small. He settled for waving his hands about instead. "If we can get Twist and the other engineers to fake the ship-seal, and Lizette to fake the scope readings, and Molly to fake the first sighting—we should be good."

He glanced at the others. Molly Cuny looked amused and a little eager for the mayhem to begin. Amelia looked concerned but calm. Pasic looked stoic as usual, his brief burst of glee already a thing of the past.

"If we do this," Demming warned, "we're stuck with it. Once we set everything in motion, we either take control from Jacobsen or get tossed back in the brig for good, all four of us, and court martialed the minute we get home."

"Assuming we make it home," Amelia reminded him. "That's why we're doing this, remember? Because if we don't stop him Jacobsen will send the *Remora* crashing into the shipyards at twice the speed of sound, killing all of us and probably anyone else nearby as well."

"Right." Demming nodded, but deep down he knew that wasn't all of it. At least not for him. Oh, self-preservation was a high priority, to be sure, and he felt responsible for the rest of the crew as well. Plus there was his general dislike of Jacobsen—he'd be happy to wipe the smug look off that arrogant bastard's face. But there was another reason he had to do this.

The mission.

The light.

They'd been sent from their world, out here into the ether, to pursue that light. To find its source and report what they'd discovered.

And something in Demming told him that their mission was a lot more than just satisfying idle curiosity. Something about that light was important. Something about what they would find would  change their whole way of life. He was sure of it, deep in his bones.

That's why they couldn't turn back. They had to keep going. They had to find out. They had to bring about that change.

And nothing could stand in the way of that.

Nothing.

He kept all of that to himself, however. He wasn't sure the others wouldn't think he was the crazy one, if he told them.

As it was, Amelia nodded. "Let's do this," she said quietly.

"I concur," Pasic added. "Too many lives are at stake not to act."

Molly Cuny shrugged. "Whatever. I just want to see you scare the squid ink out of him."

Demming clapped his hands together, rubbing them vigorously. "All right. Let's see if we can make ourselves a pirate incursion."

"Captain!" Molly Cuny called through the speaking-tube. "Captain, are you there?" Demming waited quietly, keeping as still as possible to avoid any noise giving his location away. Amelia had headed back toward engineering, saying it would be easier to talk her team into the charade in person. Pasic had stalked off toward the crew quarters to seal them in for the duration. Demming had borrowed a console in here to contact Lizette, but now he just sat quietly. This was the gunner's moment to shine.

"Affirmative," Jacobsen's voice replied a moment later. "What is it, Miss Cuny?"

"We've got a problem, Captain," she answered quickly. "A big one. I'm seeing a ship on my scope. It's coming up fast from the rear—and I recognize the outline."

There was a pause.

"Captain?" Molly Cuny asked. Demming was the only one who knew she was grinning. The only other times he'd seen the pretty little gunner's mate this excited was when she was trouncing opponents at the gym or when she was shooting something.

She was an odd girl.

"Oh, wave below," Jacobsen finally whispered. "Are you saying—is it—?"

"The *Siren Knife*," she replied. "Yes, sir."

"Captain!" Demming could faintly hear Lizette through the tube—the devices worked best when right near the mouth and the ear, and limited what ambient noise could be discerned, but the foredeck was small and the pilot was right near the captain. Plus he had a feeling Lizette was deliberately pitching her voice so not only Jacobsen but he and Molly and the rest of the officers in the foredeck could hear her clearly. "I'm picking it up as well! She's coming in fast! We're sitting ducks!"

"Permission to fire, Captain?" If he hadn't known better, Demming would have sworn Molly Cuny really did have a target approaching, she sounded so eager.

"No, no." Jacobsen's reply was practically a moan. "It won't do any good! We can't stop them! They'll come onboard again, and this time—maybe this time they came back for us! To sell us! They said we weren't worth enough, but what if they changed their mind? Or they just don't want to leave any witnesses behind?" His voice cracked, and Demming felt sorry for him. He didn't much like Jacobsen, but the man wasn't an awful person, just a bit self-centered, stubborn, and self-serving. Right now he was clearly petrified, though, and Demming found he didn't enjoy making another man quake like that. He had to remind himself that they were doing this for everyone's good. Even Jacobsen's.

"Sir, what should I do?" Molly Cuny asked. "What would you like me to do?"

At almost exactly the same time, Demming heard Lizette ask, "What are you orders, Captain?"

He almost didn't hear the sob in response, but then it came again, and again. Jacobsen had completely broken down. It was horrible to have to hear that.

Even though it was exactly what they'd be hoping for.

"Sir?" Demming recognized the slow, steady voice of Mister Dittmer. "What would you like us to do? Captain Jacobsen?"

Apparently hearing his name and rank was the last bit of coral. "Don't ask me," Jacobsen wailed, still more or less into the speaking-tube. "I can't be here! I can't be in charge! They'll kill me, don't you understand? They killed Captain Mendez and this time they'll kill me!"

"Would you like us to relieve you of command, sir?" Lizette asked, and it sounded like she was trying to keep her voice casual.

"What? Yes! Yes, relieve me of command!" Jacobsen sounded pathetically excited about the idea. "Wait, no! I have an even better idea!" Demming felt a sinking sensation blossom in his chest. He wouldn't, would he?

But apparently he would. Because the next thing he heard was Jacobsen calling through the speaking-tube. "Mister Kesselman? Mister Kesselman?"

Except that Kesselman couldn't answer. The bo'sun was still unconscious in the brig.

Wonderful.

Someone did answer, however. But instead of Kesselman's gruff but soft voice, this was sharper, crisper speaker. "Yes, captain?"

"Where is Kesselman?" Jacobsen demanded.

"Laying down—he wasn't feeling well," Pasic responded. "I gave him something to help him sleep. Can I be of assistance?"

"Fine, fine." Demming almost choked when he heard the next words: "I need you to escort Mister Demming to the foredeck at once. As fast as possible."

He was scrambling out of his seat and out of the gunnery seconds later.

The gunnery was right behind the foredeck. The brig was in front of it. Which meant he had to get past the foredeck and back to the brig before Jacobsen decided to go himself, or to send someone else, and they discovered that Demming was no longer trapped within, and that the slumbering boatswain had taken his place.

Abandoning any attempt at stealth or caution, Demming ran. His feet barely touched the gangway as he flew down its length, racing headlong past the foredeck and onward. He saw someone a ways ahead, and desperately hoped it wasn't a crewman, because there was no way he could reach the brig before that figure. But as he drew closer Demming saw that the other man was tall but slender, and with dark hair, and he relaxed. Pasic!

The doctor nodded and waved him back as he approached. "I'm to escort you to the foredeck," Pasic told him cheerfully. "Do be a good fellow and cooperate."

Demming grinned, speaking between gasps for air. "I'll do my best."

Together they retraced Demming's steps as far as the foredeck. Then they stopped. "What does he want you for, exactly?" the doctor asked, his hand on the door panel.

"The same thing we want ourselves," Demming answered. At least, he thought that's what was going on. Only one way to find out. He nodded, and Pasic activated the door.

The first thing Demming saw once it had opened was Jacobsen. The acting captain was standing between the captain's chair and the first lieutenant's, as if he couldn't decide which way to go—his old rank or his more problematic new one. His eyes were wild, his normally tight curls bouncing in disarray, his skin flushed. When he saw Demming, he started giggling.

"Ah, Mister Demming! Join me, please!" Jacobsen indicated the space near him, but on the same side as the command chair.

"I take it you're no longer angry with me?" Demming nodded to Pyle and Dittmer as he passed them and headed toward the front. Lizette was also watching him, and when he glanced her way she responded with a wink and a quick grin.

"That?" The captain waved the thought away. "Oh, that was nothing. No, I'm a great admirer, actually. You've always been so good at dealing with sudden crises—you perform well under pressure."

"Thank you." Demming was next to him now, and accepted the hand Jacobsen offered. The grip was weak and twitchy, unlike the acting captain's usual bone-crushing clasp.

"In fact," Jacobsen continued, "we have a little situation

I think you're far better suited to handle." He giggled again, but fought to get it back under control. "The *Siren Knife* has returned, it seems. And I find myself ill-equipped to deal with them." He clapped Demming on the back, and kept his arm around Demming's shoulders afterward, effectively trapping him. "Therefore, I am stepping down as captain, effective immediately. As my first lieutenant, that leaves you in command."

"Me? Oh, no." Demming knew that the best way to get something was to say you didn't want it. "I can't be captain! You're the ranking officer onboard."

"I am removing myself from the chain of command," Jacobsen replied. Even his voice seemed wobbly, thin. "That leaves you in charge. Surely you can handle it." He gave Demming a wavery grin, and more giggles erupted from between his lips.

"Are you certain this is what you want?" Demming asked him. In front of Lizette, Pasic, Dittmer, and Pyle. This was actually going even better than planned!

"Yes, I am certain." Jacobsen glanced around, realized the other officers were watching, and raised his voice to make sure he was heard. "I, Gist Jacobsen, acting captain of the HMES *Remora*, hereby remove myself from command and from any possibility of regaining command. I resign my commission as an officer, and lower myself to the rank of common seaman instead. As my acting First Lieutenant, Mister Demming is now the ranking officer on this ship, and will become its captain." He slapped Demming on the back again. "Do you accept this responsibility? Say you do!" His grip tightened.

"I do," Demming agreed quickly. He could feel his pulse racing, and he wanted to shout, but that wasn't appropriate for an officer of the line. And especially not for the new captain!

"Excellent!" Jacobsen still sounded off, and Demming realized with a start that the other man's eyes weren't completely focused. "I think it's best if I remove myself to the crew quarters, don't you, sir?"

Demming frowned. "Actually, no. I think you need to have the doctor look at you. I believe you're suffering from some form of shock." He gestured Pasic over, and the doctor moved quickly, his long strides covering the distance from the door in no time.

"I'll take care of you," Pasic assured the slightly dazed-looking former acting captain. "Come along, Mister Jacobsen."

"Mister," Jacobsen whispered as the doctor led him out. "He called me mister! I'm not a captain anymore. How excellent!"

Demming waited until the door has slid shut again behind the oddly matched pair. Then he turned and took the remaining steps to the command chair. He ran a hand along its fine leather back for a moment, admiring it. Then his hands strayed to the armrests and the seat. The captain's chair! He'd always hoped to attain one someday. But he'd never imagined it would be during his first mission! Or that it would mean commanding a ship in ether rather than water.

But there it was, and here they were, and things happened.

And right now, what was happening was him settling himself into the command chair as if he belonged there.

Which, in all honesty, he did.

Or at least he was going to work hard to convince himself of that.

"Captain?" It was Molly Cuny—Demming wasn't sure if Jacobsen had ever broken the connection before or if she had called back.

"Yes, Miss Cuny," he answered. He knew she'd recognized his voice, and that she knew exactly what it meant. He reminded himself to contact Amelia as soon as possible as well. She needed to know that they wouldn't need a fake ship-lock for their little masquerade.

He also had to work hard to repress the little shiver that went down his spine at being addressed as "Captain."

"We have a small problem, sir." Was she smiling again, back in her little gunnery?

"What problem is that?"

"That ship I mentioned before, sir?"

"Yes?" Demming knew that had just been a ruse, so he wasn't particularly worried.

"It's—well, it's real, sir."

Demming almost choked in dry air. "What do you mean, real?"

"Three thousand feet and closing, sir," Molly Cuny continued. "And the configuration is very different from the *Siren Knife*. We've got an unfamiliar craft approaching us, sir. What shall I do?"

Demming couldn't help but laugh. Well, he'd wanted Jacobsen out the way and out of command. Apparently he'd got both.

He just hadn't expected taking command to become quite so . . . involved.

And especially not in his first five minutes.

# CHAPTER SIXTEEN

"SHOW ME," DEMMING DEMANDED, LEANING forward in his new chair. It creaked beneath him, clearly used to Captain Mendez's shape and weight. He hoped he and the seat would have enough time to become accustomed to one another.

A second later, part of the foredeck's front canopy went blank. Then it cleared to reveal the atoll still towering over them on all sides. But the rocks were different from the ones he had been staring at just a moment before. This was the view from the gunnery's rear port, showing the scene behind them.

And, as Demming watched, something drifted across one of the floating cliff faces.

"That?" Pyle, still seated behind him, asked after a second. "That's a ship? It looks like a cloud!"

Demming had to agree. He'd been expecting something like the *Remora* or the *Siren Knife*, something with sharp edges and clean lines and a metallic hull. But this—it was a wisp of color, nothing more. How was that a ship at all, much less a threat?

"I'm afraid I'm not seeing it, Miss Cuny," he said into the speaking tube. "I think Mister Pyle is correct. That seems to be some sort of cloud, or ink blot, or perhaps even an etheric form of seaweed."

"Can seaweed or ink cover five hundred feet a second, sir?" There was an unfamiliar edge to the gunner's mate's voice. "Or arc over the nearest rocks and home in on our location? Because that's what it's doing. Sir."

Demming looked again, rising to step closer to the canopy. Not that those few feet made much difference at this range. But now, staring at the filmy shape again, he thought he could make out faint outlines against the rocks. Clouds could have hailstones, he knew from his surface meteorology classes. And of course seaweed could trap all sorts of shells, coral bits, and even small creatures in its clumped strands. But these—they didn't look like random fragments. Perhaps it was just Molly Cuny's statement influencing him, but Demming thought the half-hidden shapes here looked more regular than that.

And he thought he saw one of them move.

"Can we get out of here?" he asked Lizette, who was right beside him.

"Not right away," the pilot answered, never taking her eyes from the screen. "I'd need time to power up the impellers and the ram."

"What about hitting it with the ram?" Dittmer offered, proving that he'd been paying attention after all. "If it's as diffuse as it looks, one good shockwave should scatter it across the atoll."

"Good thinking." Demming spun back toward his chair and grabbed the speaking tube. "Miss Cuny, target that . . . ship with the sonic ram. Fire when ready. Full force."

"Aye aye, captain!" Her glee practically vibrated through the tube.

A few seconds went by, and the shape drew closer. Now Demming was sure the sharp-eyed little gunnery mate had been correct. This thing held its edges too cleanly to be just random gasses or stray particulate matter. And it was moving with definite purpose, approaching them but not quickly. The way an eel might stalk a fish, taking its measure and gauging its resistance before suddenly striking.

Then a light shudder shook the ship. Demming thought he could almost see the ripple of sonic energy as it spread out from the *Remora*'s forward ram generators. Ether was an excellent conductor, allowing the sound wave to pass through with no distortion at all, and he could only imagine the stunning impact that burst would have upon the cloud-like ship when it struck—

--which is why he was utterly shocked to see a flash of light spring up from the cloud's forward expanse, flickering outward in a concentric ring. Exactly like a rock thrown into a pool.

Or a sonic beam striking a hard surface and being deflected.

"They've got some kind of shield!" Pyle announced unnecessarily. The young midshipman's voice wavered. "We're defenseless!"

"Don't surrender the ship just yet, Mister Pyle," Demming warned. He let a little bite creep into his voice, knowing that edge would force the younger officer to control his fear.

Though privately Demming had to agree. There was no chance harpoons would have any effect on the mobile cloud. Their only shot had been the sonic ram. And clearly that was useless here.

He wondered for the first time if Jacobsen had been right to surrender his position. Was this another pirate ship, here to slaughter them or sell them into slavery? If so, his new rank as Captain made him the most obvious target.

He drew himself up to his full height. Well, if that was the case, he would die with dignity.

Which was small comfort.

"Orders, Captain?" Lizette asked. Her eyes were wide, so wide he could see white all around her black irises. She wanted him to come up with some clever way to save them, he knew.

He wanted that, too.

A voice broke in on his thoughts. A familiar voice, and a welcome one even at a time like this.

"Captain?" It was Amelia. "Captain, I'm picking up a strange energy burst from that . . . ship."

"An attack?" Demming asked. But something in her tone told him that wasn't the case.

"I don't think so," she answered, confirming his guess. "It's a sound wave, but not powerful enough to cause any damage. Tightly focused, though."

"Communication, maybe? Or a sonar scan?" Either would use a sharp, clear burst of energy instead of the broad wave of the ram.

"Possibly so. Do you want me to receive it?"

That was a tricky question. If it was some kind of attack, accepting the signal would allow it access to the *Remora*'s systems. What if these strangers had some way to compact sound and then expand it at will, funneling it into their receivers and then opening it out into a destructive wave?

But if that was the case, they probably had other weapons at their disposal as well. So blocking the signal would only prolong the inevitable.

But if it was communication . . .

"Accept it," he told her, flattening his palms on his armrests. He tried to project calm and confidence for the three officers watching him.

They sat in silence for several seconds, and it was all

Demming could do not to get up and run screaming from the cabin. Then Amelia's voice emerged once more.

"It's mathematics!" There was no missing the surprise or the excitement in her voice. "It's a string of numbers! They *are* communicating with us!"

Numbers! Demming vaguely remembered old tales about the early days beneath the waves, when the different clans held isolated spots within the ocean. They spoke different languages back then, and so encounters between clans usually ended in bloodshed. Until one of the earliest scientists, Tolliver Barnes, hit upon the idea of scrawling a partial mathematical formula in the sand at his feet. The other clan's scouting party stared at the numbers for a moment, before one of their older members pushed his way forward and completed the equation. That was the first time two clans had come together peaceably, and it was the beginning of what eventually became the Wavelorn Empire.

And now here were these unknown creatures out in the ether, using the same method. On them.

"Can you reply?" he asked his chief engineer.

"I think so," she answered. "But there's something strange about these numbers. They don't make any sense. Unless . . ." she trailed off.

Demming knew better than to rush her. Amelia had shown an uncanny gift of numbers and equipment back in training. It was why she'd been such an easy choice for engineer. If anyone could figure out this puzzle, she could.

Meanwhile, the cloud-ship had come to a halt a few hundred feet away from them. "It's at a dead stop," Lizette reported. "Just ceased all movement." That was the last proof. There was no way it wasn't alive, or at least occupied by something living.

Something—or someone.

"Got it!" Amelia's shout rang out through the foredeck. "It's in base-twelve!"

"Base-twelve?" Base-ten was standard, at least for them. What sort of creature used base-twelve as its root?

Demming suspected they were about to find out.

"I'm sending them an equivalent to our alphabet, but in number-form," Amelia reported, and he could actually hear her fingers clacking on the keys. "That should give them a way to communicate using actual words."

A minute passed. Then another.

"They've replied!" Amelia announced. Her voice was shaking. "They say 'we mean you no harm.'"

Demming allowed himself to relax a little. But only a little. They could be lying, of course. But it was already clear they were more technologically advanced, so why bother with deception?

"Send a message back," he ordered. "Say 'we mean you no harm either. We are sorry we attacked you. We were set upon earlier by space pirates.'"

"Gee, just tell them your life story, why don't you?" Lizette muttered, and Demming smiled. The fact that she was mouthing off meant his pilot was feeling better. Glancing behind him, he saw Pyle and Dittmer sagging with relief as well.

An answer came a moment later. "'We may be able to help,'" Amelia read out. Not for the first time Demming wished she was here instead of in engineering. "'Permission to dock and come aboard?'"

He mulled that one for a moment. Communicating with a strange, unknown species was one thing. Inviting them onto the *Remora*? That was wholly another.

Then again, they could probably blast the ship apart from a distance if that had been their goal. So what additional harm could they do boarding?

And the *Remora's* mission was not just to seek the light source. It was also to explore the ether, and find out what lay beyond their world.

He couldn't think of a better way to do that than to speak with a—seemingly—friendly race of beings that lived and moved through the ether as if it were their home.

" 'We would be delighted to receive you,'" he declared finally, leaning back in his seat and letting out a deep breath. There. The die was cast.

Now they would see what came of it.

"The cloud-ship is maneuvering closer, sir," Lizette reported, though Demming could see its sudden dart toward them for himself. "They've aligned with the main waterlock." The ship shivered ever so slightly. "Contact! They've adhered to our hull somehow." She frowned. "No sign of magnetics, or anything mechanical. They're just . . . clinging there. Like a barnacle."

"Probably best not to tell them that comparison, Miss Mills," Demming teased her. "Let's not insult our guests just yet, hm?" She stuck her tongue out at him, and Pyle laughed.

Then Demming tapped the button on his armrest that let him speak to the entire ship at once. "Your attention, please," he said slowly and calmly. "We have made contact with a new race. They have offered us assistance. We are allowing them to come aboard. Please stay in your quarters unless summoned, and do not be alarmed. They appear friendly. Repeat, they appear friendly." He hoped Jacobsen was confined to quarters, or sedated, or both.

That done, Demming rose from his chair. "Miss Mills, you have the wheel," he told Lizette as he circled his seat and headed toward the foredeck's door. Behind him, Lizette grumbled good-naturedly. "Don't worry," he assured her, "if they really are friendly I'm sure they'll want a tour of the ship. You won't be left out." He paused at the door panel. "Mister Pyle, with me." The young midshipman practically leaped to his feet.

"Yes, sir!" Pyle enthusiastic salute would have set him spinning head over heels if they'd still been underwater. Instead, he just staggered back a pace.

"Easy there," Demming warned, though his own blood was racing and he had to clench his hands to keep them from shaking. "Let's do our best to appear calm, hm?"

He tapped the panel and grinned as the door irised open, and his steps were light as he turned toward the prow and the *Remora*'s main access portal.

Time to meet the cloud-people!

# CHAPTER SEVENTEEN

DEMMING WAS ONLY A LITTLE surprised to find a tall, slender, long-braided figure waiting for him and Pyle at the forward lock.

"Miss Scutt." He tried to hide a smile but it kept twitching at his lips. "I don't remember saying I needed our engineer present for this."

"I brought you this." She thrust a small, square box at him. "It's a short-range sonar receiver. I've modified it—I programmed in the base-twelve alphabet conversion, and set it to produce those as sounds. It'll let you hear what they're saying in plain English." She didn't meet his eyes, and he suspected from her blush that it was because if she did she'd start grinning like a small child caught staying up past bedtime.

"Thank you." He accepted the receiver. "What about translating my words into something they can understand?"

She just shrugged. "I'm assuming they'll have something similar to this, so that shouldn't be necessary." She made no move to leave, and Demming didn't suggest it. Truth be told, he was happy she was there at his side.

"Very well." He tugged at his jacket, brushed a bit of lint from it, and rubbed a hand across his head. "Let's meet our guests." Then he nodded to Pyle, who typed the access code into the portal. There was a whir and a faint shudder as the outer layer cycled open, and the light on the panel changed from green to red. After a moment they heard and felt the outer door shut again, and the light flicked back to green. Pyle hit the button, and the inner door slid open as well, revealing—

Demming stared.

Beside him, he was sure Amelia and Pyle were as well.

Before them, floating out of the portal, were—well, three small clouds. Bright, colorful clouds, like the wisps of light and vibrance they'd seen out among the ether. Hints of purple and red and blue and green and orange and colors Demming didn't have names for all swirled and spun and shifted together. But at the same time he could see right through these beings, to the walls of the portal and the sealed outer door beyond. They had no eyes, no faces at all, no hands or feet, no bodies. They were clouds. Small, filmy, iridescent clouds, like the stain of oil on water.

"Greetings," the foremost of the clouds said. Demming gaped at it. The word had come from the cloud itself, not from his receiver, and it was in perfect Queen's English.

The moment stretched on silently.

Finally the cloud shifted, and flickered, its blue and green hues cycling rapidly from one shade to another. "Did we say that correctly?" It asked. "Greetings?"

Demming forced himself to recover his senses and his poise. This was a historic moment, the first meeting between humans and . . . whatever these were. He wasn't about to have it written in the histories that he stood there slack-jawed and drooling, and that their guests decided they were all idiots as a result.

"You said it perfectly," he assured them. "I apologize. We

were . . . taken aback by your appearance. We have never encountered anyone like you."

"Ah." The clouds drifted forward, and the lead one paused only a foot so from Demming's face. "You are new to etheric travel?"

He saw no reason to deny it. "Very. This is the first ship our people created that could breach the air barrier and enter the ether."

"An early exploration vessel? Fascinating!" That was from the second cloud, which glided forward a bit. It was a little larger than the first cloud, and its hues tilted more toward red and orange. "How do you feel? Are you excited? Nervous? Scared?"

"Uh, all three, yes," Demming answered. "I'm Nathaniel Demming, captain of the HMES *Remora*. This is Amelia Scutt, our chief engineer, and Benson Pyle, our midshipman." He waited.

"Ah, identifying nomenclature," the first cloud responded. "How quaint." It flickered a bit, as did its two companions. "We do not use such limiting details amongst ourselves. There is no need. We can identify one another through resonance and composition. But if you prefer labels, you may refer to me as Researcher One. This is Researcher Two"—the second cloud brightened— "and Researcher Three." The third cloud, slightly smaller than the first two, rose and twirled. Its colors were mostly yellows and oranges.

"It's a pleasure to meet you." Demming would have offered a hand to shake, but clearly that wouldn't work here. He settled for a smile and hoped they recognized that as a friendly gesture. "What sort of people are you, if you don't mind my asking?"

The three clouds had drifted further into the staging area,

and Pyle closed the portal's inner door behind them. If that alarmed them at all, Demming couldn't see it. But how would you tell, really?

"We are living clouds," Researcher One answered. "That is the translation your system provides for the mathematics that describe us, and it will suffice. And you?"

"Humans, from Earth." Demming glanced over at Amelia, who shrugged. This conversation certainly wasn't going the way he'd imagined. "You're the second strangers we've met out here. The first were pirates—from a ship called the *Siren Knife*."

"Ah, the Olsat." That was Researcher Three. "We have heard of encounters with them before. Vicious and brutal. You are lucky you survived."

"They didn't mean for us to," Pyle muttered from the rear, and even without actual eyes Demming could tell that all three clouds had just shifted their attention to him. "Thought they'd left us choking to death, they did."

"The Olsat are not usually so careless," Researcher One observed. "You say you tricked them? How did you manage this?"

Demming debated whether to answer that or not. But so far these "living clouds" seemed friendly enough, and if he wanted their help he figured he'd better humor them. "We're amphibious," he explained. "We can breathe both water and air. The *Remora* was filled with water, which the . . . Olsat? . . . siphoned off. They left us collapsed on the deck, and probably thought we would suffocate without it." He shrugged. "They were wrong."

"An amphibious race, like the Lacmupo!" Researcher Two floated closer, and hovered by Amelia's neck, clearly studying the gills there. "Fascinating!"

"We are a research vessel," Researcher One explained. "We travel the cosmos seeking knowledge, of races, ships, planets, and all else. That is why we approached you. We have never seen a ship of this configuration before."

"It's modeled after the scout ships our people use underwater," Demming told the cloud. "But modified for etheric travel."

"Yes, of course." The creature bobbed up and down in what might have been a nod and might simply have been a stray air current. "Yet your propulsion does not seem well-suited for the ether."

Amelia cut in here. 'It isn't," she admitted. "Our scientists expected the ether to have more substance to it, some mass but very low pressure. Our impellers draw particles in, whip them around, and fire them back out to give us velocity. But there aren't any particles out here—the ether is empty. So we have a hard time moving."

"We can help with that," Researcher Three offered. "We have plans for dozens of different starship engines in our idea catalogs! We could show you how to fabricate one that would be far more efficient out here in the ether!" It danced about as it spoke, and left trails of vapor behind it, like a flower shedding petals.

"We would be happy to assist you in this, and whatever else we may provide," Researcher One confirmed. "In return, we would ask that you allow us to scan both your ship and yourselves for our idea catalogs. The process is completely harmless, and allows us to add you to our store of knowledge."

"Thank you. We'd be happy to allow that, and we appreciate whatever aid you can provide." Demming hated asking for help, but he knew it was that or drift out here forever. Sometimes pride just wasn't worth it.

"Excellent." Researcher One jiggled about. "We will divide, to effect aid and absorption more quickly," it declared, and it was clear to Demming that he was the leader of the trio. "Researcher Three will work with your engineer to provide your ship with more useful propulsion. Researcher Two will scan yourself and the others aboard your ship, and will assist with any other needs you may have—I regret that we will not be able to provide water for you, but we may be able to assist with other supplies. I will study your ship itself, both to scan it and to see whether we might provide additional improvements to make your journeys safer."

Demming nodded. "I'll let the crew and the other officers know," he assured the three clouds. "We'll give you a full tour, and then Miss Scutt can work with Three in Engineering, while Mister Pyle and our bo'sun, Mister Kesselman, assist Two in the crew quarters. I'll make myself available to you as well, should you have any other questions."

He waited a second, but the three clouds didn't reply. He couldn't read their faces, of course, but judging from the soft, smooth color changes within each of them he assumed they were content with this arrangement. At least, he hoped so.

"Right," he said after a moment. "Shall we begin the tour, then?" And he stepped toward the door back out to the gangway, the three clouds floating along behind him.

Over the next few days, Demming and the others got to know the three Living Clouds fairly well. At least, as well as they could, given how different the two races were. There were only three of the clouds on their ship, which they identified as "Research Vessel 93." Obviously their race didn't bother to name its ships either, but referred to it by its function—theirs was a research and exploration vessel, designed to travel vast distances and study anything and everything it encountered. Especially unfamiliar races.

The three clouds had different personalities, Demming soon learned. Researcher One, the leader, was calm and cool and dispassionate. It only cared about knowledge, of any sort. Researcher Two was more interested in feelings and emotions, and in trying to understand other races. Demming had initially assumed that made Two younger, but he later found out he was wrong—Two was actually the eldest of the three, and had evidently moved beyond pure academic knowledge to applying that knowledge toward understanding. Three was the youngest, and still a bit flighty, prone to changing topics suddenly and randomly. Three was also the least cohesive, and bits of its cloud-stuff often floated free, especially when it was excited or agitated.

The three clouds didn't have protective suits, of course, but they did use a low-level energy field to help protect them when they were outside their own native environment. Which made sense—a good stiff current would tear the cloud-people to shreds.

Their ship was much as they were, various gasses spun together into a loose form that held its approximate shape only because the ether had no pressure, no current, and no gravity. An unfamiliar energy wrapped the ship in a translucent cocoon, and Amelia theorized that the energy was what provided them with motion, as well as defending them from harm. It had been that cocoon that had blocked the sonic ram.

Demming had apologized for that, but Researcher One had not been concerned. "We have been fired upon by many races," it explained casually. "It is natural to fear the unknown, and in your case doubly so, for you had already encountered one new race to your detriment. You were merely being cautious, a worthy survival trait."

The scans didn't hurt at all—there was a faint tickle, and his hair stood on end, but otherwise Demming didn't feel any different during or after. Some of the crew had a hard time dealing with the sight of the clouds floating down the hall— Jacobsen practically disappeared—but everyone else soon got accustomed to them, and even enjoyed their presence. The living clouds were like wise old scholars, friendly and harmless and a little bit odd. The fact that they were puffs of gas didn't change that impression much.

Amelia had perhaps the most difficult time, though she loved every minute of it. She and Researcher Three discussed engines in great depth, and went through the various sorts the clouds had seen and studied thus far. They considered the *Remora*'s existing capabilities, including her tools and her spare parts, and decided upon a particular engine as the easiest for them to create and the easiest to connect to the ship's current systems.

"It's a radiation propulsion unit," she explained to Demming and some of the other officers one evening in the officers' mess. "It turns out the one thing the ether has plenty of is radiation, energy on all sorts of levels we can't see or feel. All we have to do is reconfigure the impellers to work off radiation instead of particles. They'll draw in radiation, whip it about, churn it into a frenzy, and then forcibly eject it to send us shooting forward. Same principles, just a different fuel."

"Sounds good," Demming agreed. "And all you have to do is some minor tweaks on the impellers?"

That had gotten a laugh out of her. "Well, I wouldn't say minor, but yes—we can use most of what we have already. It just needs some modifications. Give me and my team a few days and we'll have the *Remora* flying faster than ever."

She wasn't the only person making modifications. Demming had seen Molly Cuny and Researcher Two speaking quietly on a few occasions, and chanced by the gunnery one evening to find the petite gunner's mate busy replacing circuits and wires in one of the weapons consoles.

"Miss Cuny," he said, interrupting her work, and she shot him an irritated glance but didn't pause. "Might I ask what you're doing?"

"Giving us weapons that work," she answered, her reply sharp and clear as it only was when she was talking about weapons.

"How are you managing that, exactly?"

The grin she gave him beneath her curls was a bit nasty and more than a little intriguing. "The impellers are going to run on radiation now." She shrugged. "I figured, no reason the weapons couldn't do the same."

"So you're altering the sonic lance so it fires radiation bursts instead?" Demming guessed. Her short nod told him he was correct.

"Very good, Miss Cuny," he said finally. "Carry on." She grinned again, then ignored him completely. He left quickly after that.

Amelia was spending a good deal of time with Researcher Three, and Researcher Two was keeping Pyle and Kesselman busy with its questions and requests for the crew. Researcher One spent half its time floating around the *Remora*'s exterior and the other half with Dittmer, supposedly discussing ways to restock the ship somehow. Demming spoke to the cloud-people when he saw them, but for the most part he didn't have a lot of interaction with them. He wasn't the one they needed for their work.

"Amazing stuff," Dittmer was saying one afternoon. "It's like a powder, but when you add a drop of water it instantly expands. Becomes a solid block of protein—Researcher One tried to tell me what it was but the words didn't come through right. The closest equivalent I can figure is super-condensed whale blubber."

"Cooks up easily enough," Quentin agreed, serving steaming bowls of stew for lunch. "Flavors easily, good texture—you'd never know it wasn't fresh fish. They gave us enough that we can probably make due for two, three months now. Things'll get a bit boring by the end of that, since we'll run out of everything else, but we can manage."

"Excellent." Demming took a cautious bite of stew, then smacked his lips and dove in. The cook had been right—the strange protein tasted like fresh fish. "So we have sufficient food for several months," he commented contentedly after he'd wiped his bowl clean, "and unlimited fuel, and even weapons that might prove effective against the next pirate we encounter." Or the last one, he thought but didn't say. "Sounds like we're good to move on, then."

"We should ask them about the light source," Pasic commented. Demming knew the doctor had been speaking with Researcher Two quite a bit, discussing comparative anatomies. "They might know something."

Demming wiped his lips with his napkin, then dropped it on the table. "You're right." He pushed back his chair and rose. "I'll speak to them about it now."

He found Researcher One and Researcher Two hovering in the foredeck, observing Lizette as she manned the wheel. Not that there was much to see—other than a brief test of the impellers, they had yet to move, or to leave the comparative safety of the atoll.

"Captain," the first cloud said politely as he stepped up beside it.

"Researcher One. Researcher Two." Demming cleared his throat. "I wonder if I might ask you about something? Several months back, we observed a bright light in the sky, or rather in the ether beyond the sky. That was what prompted us to travel beyond our world—we knew that it meant there were other things out here, and wanted to find out more about them. Do you know anything about that light?"

"We observed it," Researcher One confirmed, flickering to mostly green. "We recorded what we could ascertain about its distance and location, which I will provide to Miss Scutt. We do not know its precise cause, however. It seems unlikely to have been an erupting star, and too large to have been an exploding ship. I would conjecture a planet, but more than that I cannot say."

"Thank you. That gives us something to go on, at least." Demming tried to wrap his brain around the idea that an entire planet had exploded somehow, and shivered. Could something like that happen to any world? Could it happen to theirs? What could cause a whole world to burst like that? He wondered if the clouds had theories for that, but was afraid to ask. If he knew, he suspected he might never sleep again.

The three of them gazed out at the ether for a moment.

Then Researcher Two spoke. "Captain, I must tell you something."

"Of course." Demming noticed that One pulsated, almost as if warning Two to be quiet, but the second cloud continued nonetheless.

"You and your people have already encountered pirates once," Researcher Two pointed out. "I fear such run-ins may continue as you proceed through the ether."

"Oh?" Demming felt his pulse begin to race, and forced his voice to remain calm. "Why is that?" The cloud's statement didn't sound like a threat.

"This ship is large enough to make an attractive target," Two continued. "And despite the modifications we have helped provide, it is not strong enough to stand up to most pirate ships in a direct battle. Your new engines will provide you with more than adequate acceleration, however, and your ship already possesses impressive maneuverability. If you do see other pirate vessels—and there many in the ether who turn to such a trade—I would advise you to run."

Demming frowned, considering that. "Thank you," he said finally. "I appreciate your concern, and I will keep that in mind."

Researcher Two fell silent, and the three of them remained there, the lights beyond twinkling around them.

The living clouds departed two days later. "We wish you health and success," Researcher One offered as he and his two companions headed for the front portal. "May your journeys bring you knowledge and enlightenment."

"And may your travels fill your idea catalogs with new and exciting knowledge," Demming replied. From the way the three clouds brightened, flickering happily, he guessed he'd said the right thing.

"Perhaps our paths will cross again some day," Two

remarked before the inner door slid shut. "I would be interested to hear how you fare on the rest of your voyage."

"We would be happy to speak with you again, should we meet," Demming assured them. "And we thank you for your assistance, and your kindness." Then the door clanged shut, and the living clouds were gone.

A moment later, they watched through the portal as the cloud-ship detached itself from the *Remora*'s hull—a low-level electrical charge had produced a magnetizing effect, Amelia had explained—and float away. It picked up speed and rose, clearing the top of the nearest cliff, then vanished from view.

"All right." Demming let out a deep breath. "Spread the word. We've been sitting idle long enough. Time to move out."

As Pyle saluted and jogged away toward the crew quarters, Demming turned and set his steps toward the foredeck. He was eager to continue on their mission. But he couldn't stop thinking about Researcher Two's warning. There was no guarantee the next pirates wouldn't be more ruthless, and more careful to make sure he and his crew were truly and properly dead. How were they going to survive if they had to keep watching over their shoulder constantly?

An idea began to form in Demming's head. He pushed it away, but it returned, and expanded. Forced to consider it, he frowned. It made sense. He wasn't happy about it, but it might work.

He just wondered if it would mean giving up everything that made them who they were.

And whether his crew, and particularly his officers, would let him get away with it.

# CHAPTER EIGHTEEN

"Where away, Captain?" Lizette asked. She'd been waiting at the wheel when he entered the foredeck. Most of the other officers were there as well.

Demming took a deep breath. Now was as good a time to share his plans as any. At least, the first of his plans. The rest . . . they would see if it even became necessary.

"Miss Scutt," he asked after stepping to his chair and switching on the speaking-tube. "A question for you."

"Yes, Captain?" she replied at once.

"Am I correct in thinking the Researchers helped us adapt our sensors as well as our engines and weapons?"

"Yes, sir. We can now scan various types of radiation as well as sound waves, so we can "see" approaching objects, including those that would be invisible to the naked eye." She warmed to her subject, and he knew her eyes were gleaming with the excitement of a true scientist. "Also, these scanners are passive—they absorb approaching radiation traces and analyze them, rather than sending out energy like our sonar. Which means other ships won't be able to tell we're using them."

"Excellent." He rubbed at his hair. "The *Siren Knife*—do we know what sort of energy it used?"

There was a pause. "No," Amelia admitted after a moment. "But I can find out." He heard her fingers tapping on a control panel. "There are traces of the Research Vessel, which tapped electromagnetic energy in the ultraviolet range. And a few hints of our new engines, from our tests. The only other radiation traces around us are in a completely different wavelength, in the microwave range. That has to be from the *Siren Knife*."

"Good." Demming eyed his assembled officers. This was the moment of truth. "Can we follow those traces?"

Lizette, who had been lounging against the wheel, straightened to attention. Pyle went stock-still. Dittmer, stretched out in his chair, merely quirked an eyebrow, but from him that was practically a shout of surprise. Pasic frowned. And Kesselman, who was on the foredeck for once—the bo'sun surprised them all by grinning, sharp and nasty, and shouting "yes!" while pumping one fist. Then he noticed the stares his reaction had earned and straightened, blushing.

"We can, yes," Amelia agreed slowly. "It shouldn't be too hard."

"Good. Once you've worked out their path, send the data up to the helm so Miss Mills can compute our course." He tugged the front of his jacket down and met each of his officers' stares calmly but without yielding. "The *Siren Knife* took us by surprise the first time we met. We were unprepared, both for their hostility and for the demands of etheric travel and combat." He offered a tight grin. "We will not be taken so again. They murdered Captain Mendez and Mister Bixby. They stole our supplies, including our water. No one treats a ship of the line in that matter and gets away with it. We will pursue them, and strike them down without compunction. Then we will continue with our original mission." He paused. "Any objections?"

He already knew what Kesselman's answer was, and the boatswain didn't disappoint. "No, sir!" he shouted.

The sharp gleam in Lizette's eye told him her answer as well. "No, sir," she agreed crisply.

Pyle saluted. "No, sir!"

Dittmer nodded slowly. "They can't get away with it," he agreed.

Demming glanced at Pasic, and the doctor's frown deepened. "I don't approve of violence, of course," he stated. "Can't, really, in my line of work." But then his expression slid into a glare. "But those pirates are coldblooded killers. Revenge aside, it's our duty to make sure they don't hurt others."

Demming nodded. There was no question what Molly Cuny would say—she was itching for a chance to use her new toys, and the pirates would be an ideal target—and Quentin wouldn't object either. Which only left—"Miss Scutt?"

At first he thought she hadn't heard. He waited patiently. Finally, just as he was about to ask again, she spoke.

"I don't like it." Her voice was so soft he could barely hear her. "We're deliberately going after them, specifically to hurt them." He heard her sigh. "But I suppose it's exactly the same as a naval ship going after pirates under the waves. I wouldn't like that either, but it's part of the job."

Demming knew that was the closest she would be able to come toward actual approval. "Very well. Rely the data once you have it. Miss Mills, lay in the course at all speed as soon as you are able. Mister Kesselman, inform the men. There could be shipboard combat, depending upon how things go. Mister Pyle, let Miss Cuny know to ready her weapons—we'll want to hit hard as soon as the *Siren Knife* is within range." He nodded. "That will be all."

Pyle and Kesselman saluted and left at once. Pasic departed as well, saying something about making sure his medical supplies were in order. Dittmer settled back into his chair, and Lizette turned back toward the stars, waiting impatiently to throttle up and get underway. It was only after the cabin had stayed silent a full minute that Demming let himself collapse into his own chair. That had gone as well as he could have hoped.

As for the other matter . . . well, they would see.

"Captain!" The shout came over the speaking-tube while Demming was enjoying a late lunch, and he bolted from the table, almost spilling his stew in the process.

"Yes, Mister Pyle?" Pyle was on watch while Demming ate and Lizette rested. They had left the atoll several days before, and their pursuit of the *Siren Knife* had been uneventful thus far. The new engines were performing beautifully, letting them move at several times their previous speed, and after a day or two of constant, tense watch, the crew had settled into an uneasy wariness, relaxed but ready to move at any time.

"We've got a ship on the long-range scanners!" The midshipman—Demming knew he should really promote Pyle to first lieutenant, but just hadn't found the right moment— reported, a wobble evident in his voice.

"I'll be right there." Amelia had been eating with him, and she was watching him now, concerned, but Demming shook his head. "It's probably not the *Siren Knife*," he pointed out. "You and Lizette figured we had at least a week before we'd be close enough to see her, even at our current speed. Most likely it's just some other random ship. The Researchers did say there were lots of them."

She nodded, but didn't uncrease her forehead. "What if it's some other pirate?" she asked instead.

"Then we'll deal with them the way the Royal Navy deals with any pirate." He squared his shoulders and hoped he looked fiercely competent. "We have a duty to police the ether, same as the water. Those who cross us will learn that quickly enough."

He hit the door panel and slipped through as soon as the door had irised open, turning at once toward the foredeck and taking long, quick strides. Part of his hurry was a need to see exactly what Pyle had spotted, but part of it was a desire to end the uncomfortable conversation as quickly as possible. He knew Amelia didn't approve of violence, though she understood its occasional necessity. He was less opposed, and suspected the talk could have turned to argument if it had continued.

And right now he didn't need her angry at him, or himself distracted by conflict with one of his officers. Especially her.

"What've we got?" he asked the instant the foredeck's door had parted. Pyle was pacing nervously between the helm and the command chair, and all but leaped as he moved to meet Demming halfway across the cabin.

"It's a ship," the younger officer reported, beads of sweat showing on his brow. "I don't know much more than that—I called you the second I saw it."

"Fine, fine." Demming slid into the command chair and glanced at the consoles. Sure enough, the scanners showed a tiny blip there, at the very edge of their range. It was too small to make out any detail, but it was cutting across their path in a straight line, too neat to be a tumbling rock and too straight to be orbiting the nearest star.

"Is it them?" Pyle asked, his voice barely a whisper. He hovered right behind Demming's shoulder.

"I doubt it," Demming replied. "The radiation traces we're following angle off the other way." Once Amelia had isolated the *Siren Knife*'s frequency, it had been easy to follow the pirate ship's trail. The energy it used apparently wasn't common out here, so it had stood out nicely against the backdrop.

Pyle sagged against the chair in relief, then straightened, remembering his rank. "So it's just some other ship?"

"Possibly." Demming frowned, considering. "It could be a research ship, like the clouds'. Or explorers like us. They could be traders, merchants, travelers, even colonists or sightseers." His fingers tapped against his chair arm. "Or they could be pirates."

"More pirates?" Pyle gulped. The two of them were the only ones on the foredeck. "What should we do?"

That was exactly what Demming had been debating in his head. Did they go after this other ship to find out who they were? Or did they continue after the *Siren Knife*? If they detoured, would they be able to pick up the pirate ship's trail again? And would following this other ship prove worth the distraction?

He considered calling the officers together and putting it to a vote. But he was the captain now. He had to be able to make decisions on his own, otherwise his crew would never respect him. He'd made the decision to go after the *Siren Knife* in the first place, and the others had all accepted it. He had to make the choice now. And hope it was the right one.

Demming studied the scope a second longer. Then he grabbed the speaking tube. "Miss Mills, please report to the foredeck as soon as possible," he ordered. He was capable of laying in a new course himself, but Lizette was far better at it, and he didn't want to leave any room for error.

The short, curvy pilot arrived a few minutes later, still buttoning her jacket. Demming tried not to notice the tight undershirt revealed through the gap. Beside him, Pyle was less successful at not gaping, and Lizette hid a sly smile as she saluted.

"Yes, Captain?"

"Sorry to cut short your sleep," Demming answered, "but we need to change course. We have a second ship in sight, and I'd like to find out what she's about. Please plot a new course— and then map out the *Siren Knife*'s likely path, based on what we've seen so far, so that we can return to our pursuit once we've looked into this other matter."

She didn't ask any questions, just saluted and slid past him to the helm, where she began scanning the information on her display and typing calculations into her navigation console. It took her twenty minutes, but finally she glanced back over her shoulder in what was probably not intended to be a sultry look but was anyway.

"All set, captain," she reported. "At present speed we should catch the unknown ship within three days. I've mapped out the *Siren Knife*'s path as well—barring any changes in direction or speed, we should be able to go straight after her and add only a day or two to our travels."

"Excellent." He nodded. The delay was minor enough that he could be allowed to satisfy his curiosity. "Please lock in the new course." He smiled. "Then you can go back to sleep."

She gave him a quick half-pout that set his pulse aflutter, followed by a seductive wink that took his breath away. "If I hurry, my bed might still be warm," she teased, her voice low and throaty, and Demming forced himself not to react to the implied invitation. He knew Lizette did it just to mess with him, but more than once he'd wondered if her flirtatious offers were genuine. He knew, though, that if he had any hope of developing anything with Amelia, he would never try to find out.

It was difficult to ignore sometimes, though.

"I won't keep you, then," he told her instead, stoically ignoring another pout. Seeing she wouldn't get anywhere with him, Lizette sighed just a little, then set the *Remora* on its new path and saluted brightly before skipping off toward the door.

Demming deliberately did not turn to watch her go.

Two days later, he met with his officers in the officers' mess.

"We've been able to get a good read on the other ship now," he explained. "Miss Scutt?"

"It's a small ship," she reported, glancing around, "but more heavily armored than we are. Probably more maneuverable, too, but not as fast on a straight run." She'd pulled an image of the ship up on the screen that covered one wall, and now she rose to gesture at various spots. "Notice how there are energy pools here, here, and here? This one is the engine, but these two—they're most likely weapons."

"So it's heavily armed," Kesselman asked, and Amelia bit her lip before nodding.

"Yes, I think so."

"Fast, heavily armored, and heavily armed." Dittmer grimaced slightly. "Doesn't sound like a research vessel, that's for sure."

"It could be a scout ship," Demming pointed out. "Prepared for trouble without looking for any. Or it could be a merchant ship, equipped to defend itself because it doesn't have an escort." He frowned and leaned back in his chair, drumming his fingers on the table. "Or it could be a pirate ship, built to hit hard and fast and then get away clean."

"They don't have a lot of cargo space," Dittmer pointed out, eyeing the image onscreen. "So if they are pirates, they don't go for bulk cargo. Just small, easily stashed valuables."

"That's true if they're a trading ship too, though," Amelia countered. "Spices, fabrics, fine arts—they could deal in high-end merchandise, so they don't need much space. But they would need protection, because they'd be an ideal target for the actual pirates."

"Either way," Demming cut in, "we want to be careful. I think we need to find out who they are, if for no other reason than I don't like having strangers at my back. If they are pirates, though, they may see us as a target. If they aren't, they could mistake us for a threat. And they're powerful enough to do us some damage, even in self-defense."

"We can take them," a sharp voice assured. Molly Cuny sat at the end of the table, eyes fixed on the image across from her. "Our new weapons could punch right through that armor." She flicked a short, sharp grin. "One shot to the engines and they're dead in the water."

"I thought we were going to talk to them, find out who they were," Amelia asked quickly, eyes pleading with Demming. "They may not be a threat at all!"

"They may not," he agreed, "and we won't attack unless we have to. I'd much rather talk than fight. But we need to be ready, just in case." She nodded reluctantly. "Are we at full speed, or just cruising velocity?"

"We're at three-quarters," Lizette answered. Pyle was on watch again. "If I put the throttle down full, we can close with them in half a day, maybe a little less. Depends if they try to run." Her grin said she'd enjoy giving chase.

"Full speed, then," Demming told her. "No sense dawdling." She nodded and rose at once. "Miss Cuny, I want you ready on weapons—target their weapons systems, but you're not to fire unless I give the order." Her nod was more curt, clearly displeased about having to wait, but Demming knew she'd obey. "Miss Scutt, the Researchers were able to communicate with us from a distance, to assure us of their peaceful intentions. Ready a similar message—we'll broadcast it at this ship as we approach, to let them know we're coming and to tell them we mean no harm." Her smile was bright as the sun as she hurried off to take care of that.

Demming rose as well, and nodded to the remaining officers: Dittmer, Kesselman, and Pasic. "Mister Kesselman, warn the crew to be ready, just in case. Doctor, I hope we won't need your services, but better you're prepared as well. Mister Dittmer, batten down the hatches—if we need to move quickly, I don't want anything popping loose." All three nodded, and within a minute the room had emptied out.

Demming was the last to leave, watching his officers move quickly and competently about their tasks. He felt good about the orders he'd given. He hoped violence wouldn't be necessary, but they were ready if it was.

He couldn't help remembering Researcher Two's warning as he made his way down the gangway toward the foredeck. "There are many in the ether who turn to such a trade."

They were about to find out if this other ship was one of those.

Demming had a feeling the encounter could determine the *Remora*'s disposition for the rest of its travels. He just hoped the result would be something they could all live with.

# CHAPTER NINETEEN

"NEARING THE EDGE OF BROADCAST—AND weapons—range now, Captain," Lizette informed Demming as he entered the foredeck. He nodded and took his seat right behind her. Dittmer, Pyle, and Pasic were already in their places—Demming glanced over at the empty lieutenant chairs to either side and repressed a twinge of guilt. Soon. Right now they had other things to worry about.

"Do we have a clear visual yet?" he asked his pilot, and she nodded, her fingers skipping across her console. A small frame appeared around the equally tiny shape ahead of them, then expanded rapidly, overlaying the regular view of the ether racing past. In the newly enlarged window they could clearly see the ship they were closing with so quickly.

It looked as wide as the *Remora* but nowhere near as long, a shorter, more compact shape and far less streamlined. The armor plating was obvious even from the rear, as were several weapon turrets. Studying its clearly martial design, Demming had a hard time believing Amelia's theory that this was merely a trader or scoutship out to protect itself. If she were right, the ship's owners knew a lot more about etheric dangers than they did.

"We're sending our broadcast," Lizette reported, and Demming fancied he could see a faint ripple across the stars as the sonic burst sped ahead of them, targeting the unfamiliar vessel. He hoped hailing them was the right thing to do— they were surrendering any element of surprise by doing so, and given the other ship's heavy weaponry that was a tactical mistake even if it was a moral victory. Moral victors were often the ones who suffered, however—particularly in combat. And he was determined to come out on top in the event of an etheric battle.

"Now what, sir?" Pyle asked from behind him. Thanks in part to the decreased number of officers, and also his earlier promotion and increased responsibilities, the young officer had taken to asking questions more and more often. Demming didn't mind—they weren't inappropriate questions, and they were only asked when there were no regular crew present, so there was never any risk of the men seeing division among the officers, or uncertainty from their captain. Besides, Pyle's questions kept him honest.

"Now we wait," he answered, trying to keep his tone light despite the muscles jumping in his jaw. "We have no way to tell if they received our broadcast, or even if they can understand it, so we continue to close with them until and unless they contact us and ask us not to." As a precaution, however, he thumbed the switch on the speaking tube. "Miss Cuny, stand ready."

"Weapons loaded and target locked, Captain," came the immediate reply. He knew the tiny gunner's mate was leaning forward at her console, finger poised over the firing button, itching for the word to release devastation on the now-warned ship before them.

Demming still hoped it wouldn't prove necessary.

"They're accelerating," Lizette reported. "And they've changed course slightly. Looks like they're angling toward that atoll up to the right. If they can reach it, it'll provide cover—they might be able to slip through while we're still navigating the rocks, and get away before we can spot them."

"Hm." Demming considered. "Running doesn't strike me as the response of an honest ship, but it could be they're just wary of us. Or they simply like their privacy. That's certainly not a crime back home, and I can't imagine it is here. Will they be able to give us the slip?" The last was said a little more loudly, so his pilot knew the question was for her.

"Not really," she replied after a second's glance at her display. "They'll increase the time before we can close with them, but we've got the stronger engines. We should still be able to reach them before they can hide among the rocks."

Demming leaned back. "Fine. Maintain present speed, and send the message again. Perhaps when they realize we haven't attacked they'll calm down." He could understand why some ships might not want to meet anyone out here in the ether, all alone, but why not reply, at least? A simple "we hear you, please leave us alone" would have sufficed. His gut told him the other ship was acting guilty, but he didn't want to condemn them just on a feeling.

They continued to close the gap, though more slowly than before.

"Captain, I'm detecting an energy increase from the other vessel!" Amelia's voice announced suddenly from the speaking tube at his side. "Centered mid-ship!"

"Guns! They're arming weapons!" Demming slammed a fist down on his chair arm. "Abyss! They want a fight! Miss Cuny, fire!" He wasn't about to let the other ship get the drop on them, now that he knew they intended a hostile response. The *Remora* wasn't heavily armored—they'd never expected to need anything beyond hull integrity and possible deflection of small rocks and other etheric debris. If the other ship got a shot off first, it could cripple them. Or worse.

"One away!" Molly Cuny shouted back, her voice going almost shrill with excitement. "Two away!" The entire ship rocked slightly, and again Demming imagined he could see flickering shapes, narrow and diamond-headed, winging their way across the ether. A moment passed, then another. Then he saw a burst of light blossom from the other ship's midsection and a second one near its stubby prow. He didn't need Molly Cuny's thrilled report of "Direct hit! Weapons disabled!" to know that she had taken out the other ship's firing capability. An action, he reminded himself, that the other ship had provoked. Only his crew's readiness, and his gunner's being quick on the draw, had saved the *Remora* from a comparable fate.

But they weren't done yet.

"Prepare to broadcast," he ordered, and a second later Amelia confirmed that his message would be sent to the other ship. "This is Captain Demming of the HMES Remora," he announced slowly, trying to keep his anger in check and his voice measured and even. "You have fired upon us, and we have responded by disabling your weapons. We are closing the distance between us. Do not attempt to flee—we would be forced to chase you and to inflict additional damage upon your ship. If you cooperate, matters will be far easier on everyone."

Switching off the speaking tube, he sat back and waited. And waited.

"They're slowing down!" Lizette reported. "They've powered down their engines!"

"Good, they've decided to be reasonable. Close the distance, Miss Mills," Demming ordered tersely, leaning forward in his chair, one hand gripping the armrest, the other still clenched in a fist and balled near his chest. "Let's board our new friends and find out why they were so eager to respond to our hail with first escape and then violence."

"Aye aye, captain." Lizette's hand was steady on the wheel, her gaze locked on the ship ahead. "We'll be on them in ten minutes."

"Mister Kesselman," Demming called to the crew quarters.

"Aye, sir?"

"Ready a boarding party, yourself and ten men. Standard armaments, but no attacks unless necessary. Mister Pyle and I will meet you at the forward port."

"Yes, sir."

Demming could feel the eyes upon him, and was unsurprised when Pasic spoke up. "You're boarding the ship, captain? Are you sure that's wise?" He knew the doctor's use of his rank was deliberate, to remind him of his duties to the ship and crew.

But Demming was determined. "Maybe not," he admitted, rising to his feet. "But I ordered that ship fired upon. I'm responsible for our disabling it. I need to see with my own eyes that I made the right decision, and to gauge their disposition before I can determine how best to conclude our dealings with them."

He saw Pasic consider that, then nod, and tried to hide his relief. As the ship's doctor, Pasic was the one man who could question his authority, and even his fitness to command. Plus, Demming respected the tall, slim medical man's opinion. He knew he could give Pasic an order and expect it to be obeyed unless it directly contradicted either the doctor's healing oath or the obvious safety of ship and crew, but he preferred to have the man's approval as well.

"Mister Dittmer, you have the watch," Demming informed his quartermaster formally, and Dittmer rose to his feet and saluted as briskly as he could, which wasn't much less casual than his usual. But Demming knew the tall, lazy-eyed man well enough by now to know the *Remora* would be in good hands while he was gone. He didn't really expect any trouble, but after their dealings with the *Siren Knife* he knew it was better to be prepared.

"Ready, Mister Pyle?" he asked as he stepped toward the door, and the young midshipman fell in beside him.

"Ready, sir!" The door cycled open, and together they headed toward the forward lock and their first encounter with yet another ship.

Clean. That was Demming's first impression of the other ship as he stepped through the joined portals—there had been no further signs of resistance as Lizette piloted the *Remora* in close, then turned her so neatly her hull just barely brushed the other ship's exterior, her forward lock grazing the similar circle along the disabled vessel's side. Nor had there been any outcries when they had used an electromagnetic pulse—a trick they'd learned from the Researchers—to adhere their ships together, so that they could then bond the two locks tight enough to prevent air from escaping into the ether when they stepped through. The royal scientists had assured them during their training that any such breach would be instantly fatal, due to the extreme low pressure all around, and Demming took them at their word. Fortunately, Amelia had been able to determine by use of various scans that the other ship bore a similar atmosphere to their own, and so the locks had faced air and comparable pressure on both sides. Still, he breathed a sigh of relief as he set foot on the other ship's deck and confirmed that the air, though tinny, was otherwise normal.

And the ship was very clean.

No, not clean, exactly. Empty. Utilitarian. He hadn't expected wood paneling and oil paintings, of course, but there were no decorations here at all, nothing but bare metal walls and grid-patterned metal floors and dimly glowing ceilings. The *Remora*, at least, had a pleasing mosaic design inlaid in the walls, its pattern both pleasant and directing crew toward various rooms through subtle color cues. This ship looked as if it had already been stripped bare of all but the strictest essentials, and yet Demming suspected it had been built that way from the start. It didn't strike him as a pleasant way to live.

Then again, the crew didn't strike him as particular pleasant, either. They were arrayed around the central cabin when he and his boarding party arrived—they already knew from Amelia's scans that the lock opened into the largest chamber, from which smaller rooms protruded on each side. Judging by the metal table bolted to the floor off to one side, and the matching benches on either side of it, this room was both a mess hall and a meeting chamber. It might serve other purposes as well, but if so Demming wasn't seeing any sign of them just yet.

The ship's crew had chosen to meet them here, which at least suggested they were going to be cooperative. Amelia had checked the ship as thoroughly as she could from the *Remora*, and had confirmed that there were only ten heat signatures aboard, meaning either the ship had a crew of only ten or it had other members who were somehow shielded from view. Demming hoped it was the former—he didn't relish the idea of walking into an ambush, or of having to tear the smaller ship apart looking for hidden crew.

Those waiting for them struck him as typical career sailors, not Royal Navy but fishermen, trawlers, shrimpers, and the like. They appeared to be men, if men were as wide as they were tall and covered in shaggy fur with long snouts and tufted, triangular ears set high. They looked uniformly surly and a bit unsavory, rough and unwashed and generally unpleasant. Their clothing was mismatched, save a dark green sash around the waist and a matching cloth cap, and all of them bore blades and pistols of various designs, though none of those were drawn.

Yet.

"What do you want?" A man in the middle demanded as soon as Demming had entered. "You pirates, looking to rob us? If so, you're out of luck—we've been hit already this trip, nothing left of value."

"You should have received our message," Demming replied, stepping forward to study the other ship's apparent leader more closely. "We meant you no harm."

"No harm?" That got a rough laugh from the other man, which his crew echoed. "You turned our guns to slag and you didn't mean us any harm? Good thing you weren't out to hurt us, then!"

"You were preparing to fire upon us," Demming pointed out, letting an edge creep into his voice to show he was not to be trifled with. "Our attack was self-defense, and we avoided piercing your hull or damaging your engines. So yes, we meant you no harm." He let the past tense of that statement speak for itself.

"Aye, well, whatever you meant, you've got us now," the other man groused. "So what're you planning to do with us?"

He crossed thick, hairy arms over his broad chest and leaned back against the wall, only his narrowed eyes and half-bared fangs putting a lie to his casual pose.

"That will depend upon you," Demming answered. "Let's introduce ourselves, at least. I am Captain Demming of the HMES *Remora*. And you are?"

"Eder Finn, captain of the *Houndstooth*," the other man admitted grudgingly. "Fine, so now we're on a first name basis, eh? Or close enough. What's next, tea and biscuits?" That got another laugh from his men, and a scowl from Pyle and Kesselman.

"Somehow I don't think that would work," Demming mused aloud, laughing along with the joke. "What manner of ship is this, Captain Finn? I haven't seen its like before." He was still trying to reconcile the weapons and armor with the complete emptiness within.

"She's a courier," Finn answered proudly. "Fast and fleet, small enough to slip in places but tough enough to survive a fight." Then he remembered his current situation, and his lips pulled back in a snarl. "At least she was."

"A courier. Interesting." It would explain her configuration, Demming thought, glancing around again, and perhaps even her sparse interior. Couriers were built for speed, and lacked most luxuries. Something still felt off, however.

"I think we'll look around, if you don't mind," he announced, striding toward the nearest door. "Just to satisfy our curiosity. If everything's as you say, we'll do what we can to patch you back up and take our leave. Fair enough?"

He was still a few paces from the entryway when he caught movement from the corner of his eye. One of Finn's crew had slipped behind the others and sidled closer to the same portal, crouched low and moving silently on the hard metal floor. His hand had dipped to his side and was now down against his flank, clutching a long, wicked-looking knife so that the blade was back against his forearm. Demming had trained enough— and seen enough tavern brawls working with his grandfather— to recognize an experienced knife-fighter readying a strike.

Demming didn't stop to think. He lengthened his stride, covering the remaining ground in the blink of an eye, and drew his diving knife from his boot as he did. At the last second he veered from the still-closed door, twisting to the side and lunging with both arms extended. His speed and altered course caught Finn's crewman by surprise, and the hairy little man found himself boxed in suddenly, one of Demming's arms snaking around his neck while the other laid the diving knife's keen edge across his throat.

Everyone froze.

"I'd drop that knife, if I were you," Demming warned quietly, his words carrying in the silence. The other man didn't hesitate, and the blade clattered at their feet a second later. "Much better. Now hold out both arms. Mister Kesselman, if you please."

The bo'sun didn't have to be told twice. He had a pair of manacles off his belt and wrapped around the *Houndstooth* sailor's forearms and wrists in a matter of seconds, the flexible braided seaweed tightening from the man's own body heat. Demming sheathed his knife, lifting the other man's weapon from the deck as he did, and stepped away a pace, putting the wall at his back and the door to his side.

"Nasty piece of work, this," Demming commented, holding the knife up to eye level so everyone could see it. It was longer and broader than his diving knife, with a curving blade that flared out near the tip. There was only one thing a weapon like this could be for, and that was for killing other men.

"I suppose we'd better have your weapons, to prevent any more unpleasantness," he declared, allowing himself to look disappointed. "Toss them to the deck in front of you, if you please." When no one moved, he nodded to Kesselman. At once the bo'sun's sonic pistol was in his hands and aimed at Eder Finn's gut. The *Remora*'s sailors had their rifles aimed at the *Houndstooth*'s crew a moment later.

"Fine, fine," Finn agreed after a brief, tense pause. "Throw 'em down, lads. No sense getting ourselves killed over nothing." He drew his own dagger and pistol and dropped them in front of him, and his men followed suit, though with much grumbling. Soon a pile of hand weapons had accumulated on the deck, and Kesselman signaled one of his men to collect them. Demming stuck his confiscated knife in his own belt, practically daring Finn to say anything about it. The other captain growled but didn't otherwise respond.

"Much better." Demming nodded, then turned to glance at the door beside him. "Now, what was it about this particular door that made your man try to attack me, I wonder? Is there something behind it you don't want us to find, or is it simply that he didn't want us wandering your ship in general?" He gave them his sharpest grin. "Let's find out, shall we?"

And he hit the door panel.

The door opened with a hiss and a burst of steam, far louder and slower than the *Remora*'s own mechanisms. Beyond was a smaller chamber, a storeroom by the look of it—shelves lined the walls, most of them bare but with a few small crates and boxes and cans here and there. Otherwise the room was as empty and unadorned as the main cabin.

Demming shook his head. "He was afraid I'd steal your last can of soup?" he asked Finn. "Really? Hardly worth killing over, don't you think?" He paused deliberately. "Unless that's not all that's in here. Is it?" He glared at the other captain, but Finn wasn't giving anything away.

No matter. Demming already had a good idea what he'd find once he looked.

"Do you know what this is?" he asked, plucking a small box off his belt. It was the same device Amelia had handed him for speaking with the Researchers. Only she'd modified it somewhat since then. "This is a handheld scanner," he explained now, waving it about. "It uses sonar—sound waves—to map out an area. The thing about sound waves is, they can actually go through most materials. Even some metals. So I can see what's in a room without having to set foot inside. Even things that're hidden from view." Finn tensed. "Let's see if you've got any more soup laying about."

And he swept the room with the scanner, switching it on to full power.

Even as he swung the device in a slow, steady arc, he kept an eye on Finn. The hairy little captain looked ready to convulse, his long jaws were clenched so tight, and his eyes had all but disappeared beneath his heavy brow. When a growl escaped him, Demming stopped and glanced back at the small storeroom—and at the wall his scanner was currently facing.

"Well, well, well, what have we here?" he asked. "Mister Pyle, why don't you and one of the boys take a look, hm? It looks like a hidden compartment to me." Finn's involuntary twitch told him he was right.

Pyle nodded and stepped into the storeroom, a sailor named Mathis at his side. They headed straight to the wall Demming had indicated, and began running their hands all along it.

It only took a few minutes before Pyle grinned and pressed harder on a spot his palm had just slid across.

The click was barely audible, but no one could miss the way a large panel suddenly popped free.

Behind Demming, Finn and his unbound crewmen stiffened, and a few tensed as if ready to lunge. A wave of Kesselman's pistol stopped them cold, however. There was nothing the *Houndstooth*'s crew could do but watch and growl as Pyle and Mathis pried the panel away completely, revealing a cozy little nook—

—filled to the brim with bottles, flasks, canteens, and other liquids containers in various shapes and sizes.

"Not soup," Demming noted aloud. "More like brandy, I'd guess, or something equally potent—and equally regulated. You're smugglers." He dropped all pretense and scowled at Finn. "Which makes you criminals. We don't much care for your kind, Captain Finn. Mister Kesselman, bind all of them securely. It's time we inspected this vessel properly."

Two of the crew tried to put up a fight, lashing out with fists and teeth, but Kesselman subdued one with a quick burst from his pistol and the other with a smart rap to the forehead from the pistol's butt. None of the others offered any resistance, but their eyes all threatened bloody murder.

"You've no right!" Finn claimed, practically howling as he was forced to his knees, arms bound behind him. "Those are our goods, bought fair and square! You're the ones stealing here! You've got no authority over us!"

"Oh? So if we took these decanters and bottles to wherever you were heading, we could sell them openly?" Demming asked. He laughed, but none of the *Houndstooth*'s men joined in. "Admit it, Finn—you're nothing but a lowdown smuggler. We've dealt with plenty of your kind in the Royal Navy. The only thing separating you from thieves and pirates is opportunity." He turned his back on Finn then, no longer interested in speaking with him. Instead, Demming supervised the thorough inspection of the *Houndstooth*.

At least the smuggling ship wasn't to blame for the crimes of its owners.

Over the next three hours Kesselman and his men scoured the *Houndstooth*, with Pyle and Demming's assistance. They found three more caches, one containing more liquids, one containing some sort of dried flowers Demming suspected were drugs, and one holding an impressive collection of coins, gems, bolts of fabric, and other clearly valuable items. They also found additional food, though they couldn't identify much of it. And there was a small barrel of slightly brackish, tinny water.

"Take what you want, but leave us something, for pity's sake!" Finn shouted, glaring as he watched them wrestle the barrel into the central chamber to join the rest of what they'd discovered.

"We're not murderers," Demming replied sharply. "Nor are we thieves. We don't want any of your goods, ill-gotten or otherwise." He gestured toward the items, which had been separated into two piles. "The food and water we'll leave here. The rest is contraband, and will be ejected." Several of Finn's men spat out what he took for curses at the news. "We'll remove your bonds as we leave, though of course I'll have men covering you from our ship in case you try anything. We didn't touch any of your tools, so you should be able to repair the damage to your weapons at least well enough to defend yourselves in

a pinch. Your engines are completely unharmed, as is the rest."
Amelia had confirmed that, slipping aboard for a quick look
at the *Houndstooth*'s systems. She'd exited the central cabin
quickly when Finn and his men—and it was an all-male crew,
Demming had noticed—had started making rude comments
toward her. Two of the boarding team were also female, and
they had looked ready to start shooting until Kesselman gave
them both a stern look. Demming suspected if he left those two
to cover their retreat Finn and his boys might experience a few
incapacitating wounds before the doors were sealed shut again.

He was debating whether that would be such a bad thing.

Finn had been right about one thing, after all. They had no
real authority here. Back home, Demming could have taken the
*Houndstooth*'s men prisoner and brought them back to stand
trial. But he wasn't even sure there were authorities in the ether,
much less how to find them. And he had no desire to lug the
murderous smugglers about indefinitely. The best he could do
was issue a stern warning, dispose of their illegal goods, and
hope they would think twice next time.

He suspected it wouldn't do much good, but it was the
closest he could come to performing the duties for which he
had been trained.

"Mister Pyle, start the return to our ship, if you please,"
Demming ordered, and his midshipman nodded and led the
way back to the *Remora*. Kesselman had his sailors following
behind, all but two who started removing manacles while their
fellows covered them from a safe distance. Finn and his men
snarled and snapped but didn't try anything.

Demming watched from beside the door as well. He knew
he should have gone back first, but he wanted to make sure the
rest of his crew departed safely.

All of Finn's men were free again save one—the same one who'd drawn a knife on Demming in the first place. As Mathis removed the manacles, the sailor lashed out with one hand and grabbed Mathis by the wrist. A quick twist and he had Mathis in a headlock, his free arm snaking around to the club Mathis had slung at his belt. That soon replaced his arm, and the sailor rose to his feet, the short length of wood hard against Mathis's windpipe.

"Try anything and I crush his throat!" the sailor warned, his voice low and savage. "Toss me a gun! Now!"

Finn took advantage of the confusion to lunge forward, toward the other *Remora* crewman still retreating with the rest of the manacles. But Demming had been watching the other captain, and he lashed out with one boot, catching Finn hard just behind one knee. The smuggler staggered and went down, clasping that leg and whimpering in pain.

"You wanted a gun?" Demming asked softly, drawing his own pistol and leveling it at the belligerent sailor's head around Mathis. "I have one right here. Now let him go." Behind him, the other crewman hurried through the portal to safety. Kesselman had his pistol raised as well, and was covering the other sailors, who were starting to edge toward them.

"Drop it or I kill him!" the sailor snarled again, tightening his grip so Mathis's face turned bright red. "I know your type— you can't let one of your own die!"

"You're right," Demming admitted, thinking fast. He lowered his gun and straightened. Then he released the trigger array and reversed his grip on his weapon. He took a step forward and held it out. "Here. Now let him go."

The sailor studied the gun warily, looking for a trick, his eyes darting about in every direction, taking in Kesselman and the riflemen behind him. "Get them back!"

Demming waved the bo'sun away, back toward the *Remora*. Kesselman glowered but complied, taking his men with him.

Now Demming and Mathis were the only ones still on the *Houndstooth*. Finn was still crumpled in a heap on the floor, but the rest of his crew began circling Demming, grinning and licking their lips.

"You wanted a gun," Demming repeated. "Here it is. Let him go. You don't need him anymore."

The sailor laughed, a nasty, deep chuckle. "Maybe you're right. Who needs him when I've got your gun—and you?" With a quick shove he sent Mathis stumbling away, and at the same time he bolted forward to snatch the gun from Demming's hand. In seconds the pistol was aimed squarely at his head.

"What's to stop me from killing you right now and taking your ship and everything on it?" The sailor demanded, showing his fangs in a wide, hungry grin. " Especially that woman who came through here."

Demming forced himself to keep calm. "Nothing," he admitted. "Except for the fact that you probably can't shoot straight even from this distance."

He watched the sailor's eyes narrow. "What did you say?"

"I said I'm not worried because I doubt you can hit me, even at this range," Demming repeated. "In fact, I'm probably the safest person in this room right now." He heard movement behind him and knew that Kesselman was readying some kind of charge, but waved the bo'sun off. "Go ahead. Shoot. It's your neck, not mine."

"You're mad!" He could see anger warring with sudden confusion and a little concern in the sailor's beady yellow eyes. Then anger won out. "Mad—and dead!"

Demming saw the sailor's arm tighten as his finger tightened on the trigger.

*Zam!*

The sonic pistol fired—and the recoil knocked the sailor's arm back so hard it slammed him in the jaw, stunning him. The weapon went flying. Demming had already dived to the floor; he rolled and came up with his diving knife in one hand and the sailor's own fighting blade in the other.

What greeted him, however, wasn't the surge of angry sailors he'd expected.

Instead he saw them all tumbling into one another, trying to flee the room—

—and the strange hissing sound emanating from the far wall.

"Captain!" Pyle shouted behind him from the *Remora*'s open hatch. "The shot pierced their hull! We've got to cut loose!"

Demming didn't need to be told twice. In an instant he was on his feet and sprinting toward the portal. A hairy blur lunged out from one side, but he lashed out with the knife in that hand and Finn staggered back, clutching at the deep slash to his chest.

Then Demming was through the linked portals and bursting into the *Remora*'s forward chamber, Pyle and Kesselman hauling him the last few feet across.

"Sealing the hatch!" Pyle shouted, hitting the access panel. The door irised shut at once, closing with a welcome thud, and the hissing vanished. So did the lightheadedness Demming hadn't noticed until it was gone.

"Separating the ships!" Pyle added, tapping in the commands, and there was a ringing clang as the *Remora* drifted free from the *Houndstooth*.

"Miss Mills!" Demming called, regaining enough strength

and presence of mind to grab the speaking tube. "Get us out of here!"

"Yes, sir!" came the reply. The ship shuddered a second later as her engines came to life, and then Demming felt a faint thrum as the *Remora* pulled away from the *Houndstooth* and put distance between itself and the floundering smuggler ship.

Demming stared out through the portal, watching the *Houndstooth* drift away behind them, sent tumbling by the *Remora*'s departure. The other ship's lock was still open, and he could see a stream of air venting from that and the smaller hole off to one side where the sailor's wild shot had gone through. He remembered what the royal scientists had said, and the times he'd seen men get the bends. He also knew that, with the hull pierced, the entire ship had probably lost integrity. Even sealing off one section wouldn't save them for very long. And once the lightheadedness and shortness of breath kicked in, it would become almost impossible to accomplish anything else. Nor was there anywhere they could turn for help—nowhere except the *Remora*, which had every reason to spurn such a request, for its own safety.

Unless they could get to their tools and repair that damage quickly, Finn and his sailors were in for a horrible, horrible death.

"Are you crazy?" Kesselman was shouting as Demming turned away from the portal and his view of the doomed ship. "He could have killed you back there!"

"Not easily," Demming answered, though he no longer felt any pride at the gambit he'd pulled. "I separated the trigger array before I passed him the gun."

Beside him, he felt Pyle stiffen, and saw Kesselman's eyes go wide. "But that—"

"I know." Their sonic pistols were designed to come apart for maintenance and cleaning. The trigger arrays were a discrete piece that could be removed. They had to be locked back into place afterward, however. Otherwise the pistol's recoil dampener wasn't properly aligned. Trying to fire a pistol like that meant it would kick as it fired, making the shot go wild and most likely breaking the shooter's arm in the process.

Kesselman shook his head. "Nice," he admitted. He slapped Demming on the back. "You really were the safest man in the room!"

"I really was," Demming agreed quietly. He glanced back once, toward the window. The *Houndstooth* was already only a small speck against the ether. "And I'm the only one to come away alive."

He didn't feel much like celebrating as he left the chamber and headed back toward the foredeck. He'd saved his ship and his crew, but he'd cost an entire other ship's crew their lives. True, they'd been smugglers and thieves and most likely murderers, but they had been men nonetheless. Finn and his crew might have deserved such a grisly fate, and certainly their treachery had brought it on themselves, but that didn't mean their deaths didn't weigh him down with every step. Demming suspected they always would.

# CHAPTER TWENTY

"WHERE TO NOW, SIR?" LIZETTE asked as Demming stepped back onto the foredeck. Her tone was matter-of-fact but he could see the sympathy in her gaze for just a second, before she turned back to the helm. Dittmer nodded to him as he made his way slowly to his chair. So did Pasic. Craddick was in his own seat, and the young ensign saluted when Demming happened to glance his way. That simple act, and the quieter but just as clear gestures from the others, made his eyes swim. His officers were telling him that they understood. None of them were blaming him for what had happened to the *Houndstooth*.

Of course, he had not yet spoken to the one whose opinion mattered to him the most. He wasn't sure he could face her yet.

"Find me the *Siren Knife*, Miss Mills," he ordered instead, once he was safely ensconced in his chair and had enough control back to speak without his voice wavering. "It's time we dealt with those cutthroats once and for all."

"Aye aye, sir!" She tapped in the new course, calling up the projected location of the pirate ship and the path she had plotted to intercept it, and brought the wheel around, curving the *Remora* in a gentle arc to follow their new course. Then she put the throttle down, the hum of the engines increasing as their ship leaped forward, eager to locate its prey. Demming himself was just as eager, both to return to that objective and to put the recent incident far behind him.

"Miss Cuny said she'll have the new weapons up and running in a few hours, captain," Dittmer announced quietly, his deep voice carrying easily across the small cabin., and Demming's attention snapped to the heavyset officer at once.

"New weapons? What new weapons?"

The quartermaster had the decency to look surprised. "She took the *Houndstooth*'s guns while you were inspecting the interior. Didn't you authorize that?"

"Not directly, no," Demming admitted, considering it. "But I did say we were going to inspect the ship and look for anything useful. I should have ordered it, actually—I just wasn't considering the possibility that we might find their guns useful, especially after we destroyed them."

"Turns out we didn't destroy the guns themselves, though," Dittmer explained. "Miss Cuny took out their power supplies instead. She said once she mounted them on the *Remora* and tied them into our systems, they would be as good as new."

Demming nodded. "Does she need help with them?"

This time the quartermaster looked a little embarrassed. "I think she already got help, sir." The heavyset man's already ruddy face darkened further. "She, uh . . . talked several of the lads into assisting her. Sir."

Demming actually laughed at that. Of course she had! Molly Cuny usually ignored any advances—or worse—but with her trim little figure and pretty features she could sway any man on the ship if she wanted. And she clearly wasn't above using that when it came to her precious weapons. Well, good for her. He was happy to see her coming out of her shell a little, even if it was only to manipulate a few crewmen into helping her attach new weaponry to the ship.

"I'll remind her to inform you once the new weaponry is active," Dittmer continued, seeing from his captain's expression that their gunner's mate's actions were not going to be a problem. "Shouldn't take more than a few hours at this point."

"Good, good." Demming rubbed the top of his head. "Miss Mills, do you have an estimate on catching the *Siren Knife*."

"Without knowing their exact speed, I can only guess, sir," she answered over her shoulder, eyes intent on the ether racing past their prow, "but I'd say between two and three days."

"Excellent." He levered himself up and out of his chair. "Keep me posted if there are any changes. I think I need a quick shower, some hot food, and a long nap." They'd had to do without real showers since the pirates had taken their water, of course, but their showers actually consisted of steam-jets that heated the water and directed it, so Amelia and her crew had adjusted the showerheads to produce simple hot air instead. Not quite as pleasant, but it got the job done.

Thinking of Amelia, Demming knew he had a stop to make before he could head toward his quarters. Once the door had shut behind him, he turned his steps toward engineering instead.

"Thank the Wave you're okay!" Amelia rushed toward Demming as he stepped into engineering. Her team glanced up, saw who it was, saluted quickly, and then just as quickly found other things to occupy them as their boss pushed past them. She threw her arms around Demming, surprising him, and hugged him tight for a second. Just as he was starting to enjoy the feel of her long, lithe body pressed against him, she let go, stepped back, and shoved him in the shoulder. "What in the Abyss were you thinking? You could have gotten yourself killed!"

"I wasn't thinking much of anything," he admitted, rubbing his shoulder where she'd pushed him. She was stronger than she looked! "They grabbed Mathis, and I knew I had to get them to let him go somehow. I just did the first thing that came to mind."

"Handing one of them your gun and goading him into shooting you?" He watched her fists bunch, and half-expected her to slug him, but then she took a deep breath and let it out slowly and deliberately. "Yes, I know you disengaged the trigger array. That was clever. But at that range he could have hit you anyway!"

"He could have," Demming agreed. He was perversely enjoying Amelia's anger. It was the most worked up he'd see her since the pirates had killed Captain Mendez and Mister Bixby, and he realized it was only because she cared about him. That discovery sent a wave of pleasure through him, and he had to struggle not to let it show as a grin. That would only make her madder. "I had to take that chance," he said instead. "I couldn't let him hurt one of my men. Or gain access to the *Remora*." He shuddered at the thought of what those smugglers would have done if they'd gotten onto this ship. He was certain things would not have ended as mildly as they had with the pirates of the *Siren Knife*.

"Well, it was stupid," Amelia told him, punching him in the same shoulder. Ouch. "Don't do it again. You're the captain—you need to stop putting yourself at risk." He suspected "you're the captain" wasn't what she really wanted to say, and had to keep himself from grinning again. Maybe he should put himself in danger more often!

"I'll be careful, I promise," he assured her. He didn't bother to point out that they were currently racing after the *Siren Knife*, and would be attacking that pirate ship as soon as it was within range. Amelia was by no means stupid. She already knew where they were heading next, and why.

"I'm going to grab a shower and some food," he explained, waving toward the door behind him. "Care to join me?" Her eyes widened and a flush stole across her pale cheeks, and he realized what he'd said. "For food, I mean!" But he couldn't help a little bit of a grin from twitching at his lips.

"I'd love to," she answered softly, holding out her arm. And as he hooked his arm through hers and turned to lead her back toward the officers' mess, Demming wasn't sure which offer she was accepting.

"I've got the *Siren Knife*, sir," Pyle reported as Demming entered the foredeck. It was the second day of their pursuit, and Lizette had reluctantly relinquished control of the helm so that she could get some much-needed rest herself, though she'd made Demming promise to wake her the minute they started to close with the pirate ship. Everyone had spent the past two days in a state of constant taut alertness, and Demming had insisted that everyone get some rest and some food whenever possible, though he knew that would only help so much. They all knew the *Remora* was hurtling straight toward another battle, and this time against foes they already knew had no compunctions against coldblooded murder.

"Show me," Demming ordered as he took his seat. He could tell from the midshipman's tone—and once again he reminded himself that he needed to promote the young officer to first lieutenant, and soon—that they weren't going to close within weapons range any time soon.

Pyle obediently punched a few buttons, and a targeting box appeared on the forward screen. It encircled what appeared to be a mere speck, but then magnified. And again. By the time the box filled most of the screen, Demming could just make out the rough outline of the bristling pirate vessel.

"Energy traces match those of the *Siren Knife*," Pyle continued, "and it's right along the course Miss Mills projected for it. It's got to be our quarry, sir."

Demming nodded. "Good work, Mister Pyle." The younger officer beamed at the compliment. "Keep us steady. Are we overtaking her?"

"Yes, sir. Her speed seems to be perhaps half ours, though that could mean she's idling rather than running at maximum. We're set to intersect her path in roughly eight hours."

"Good." Demming leaned on one arm and tapped the speaking-tube controls. "Engineering."

"Here, sir," Amelia answered at once. He hoped the flush he felt at her voice wasn't obvious to the others on the foredeck. He hadn't had the luxury to pursue the matter of the pretty engineer's possible interest since the *Houndstooth* incident, but they had dined together twice in the interim and Demming was fairly certain there was something beginning between them. Now was not the time to think on it, however.

"Is there any way to guess at the *Siren Knife*'s sensor range?" he asked instead. "I know we never got a close look at her, but I'd like to keep us just beyond her view, if possible."

"I can't be certain what she'd got," Amelia replied, her tone indicating that she was mulling it over on the spot. "From what we saw of her originally, and from our encounter with the

*Houndstooth*, I'd guess we have better range than she does. She was set up for short-range ambush in the atoll, not for pursuit across the open ether." He could almost hear her shrug. "That's just a guess, of course. I'd also suspect most of her sensor arrays are along the front, so if we come at her from behind that should give us a little more time to close before she spots us."

"Excellent. See if you can glean anything further from your readings as we approach," Demming instructed. "If we can get the element of surprise, we'll take it." He still suspected they might need it.

Next he called the gunnery. "Miss Cuny?"

"Captain." She already knew what he was going to ask, and didn't wait for him to get the words out. "We're still out of firing range, sir, but I've begun target acquisition. I'll let you know the minute we're close enough to cut through their armor." Her words were crisp and clear again, showing that she was back in combat mode, which was fine. Demming knew they would all need to be in that mindset soon.

"Thank you, Miss Cuny. Check in with Miss Scutt to make sure she's patching the latest sensor readings to your station, and keep me posted."

He closed the connection and leaned back, taking a deep breath. Soon. Very soon. They would reach the *Siren Knife* in eight hours, Pyle had said. They would probably be within weapons range sooner than that. Of course, that meant trading blows from a distance, and it meant their weapons would have less impact on the other ship's heavier armor. If only there were a way to get closer—

"Mister Pyle!"

The midshipman jumped slightly. "Sir!"

"Scan the area just beyond our projected intersection point.

I want any sort of cover you can find—rocks, gas clouds, anything."

"Yes, sir!" He could see the younger man's lips curving in a nasty smile as Pyle realized what he intended. For a second Demming considered summoning Lizette, but he knew she needed her rest. He'd want her sharp for the actual maneuvering. There was no reason Pyle couldn't handle this part, and it would be good experience for him.

Assuming they survived.

"Nothing there, sir."

That was disappointing, until Demming thought about it. Anything close to the pirate ship's path would probably be too close—they'd be spotted approaching it. "Expand your search," he ordered. "Sweep ahead and to the sides, anything that they'll cross or that could cross them."

"Aye aye, sir."

Would there be anything out there? He had no idea. The ether always seemed so empty, but that was in part because it was so mind-numbingly vast. They'd passed plenty of small rocks and the like on their journey thus far. He just hoped they'd get lucky enough to find another now.

"I've got a small cluster of rocks, sir," Pyle reported after a few minutes. "Roughly three hours out from our intersection point. Not stationary like the atolls, either—this is more like the edges of a coral reef after they're swept out by a wave, loosely grouped and moving with some speed."

That could be perfect. Demming studied the screen, where Pyle had already helpfully marked his new find. "Which way are they moving?"

The midshipman's smile widened. "Right across the *Siren Knife*'s projected path, sir."

"Excellent." He felt an answering grin stretch across his face. "Plot a course—I want us circling around to that cluster before they're anywhere near that ship. We'll slide in among them, use them for cover, and strike before the pirates know we're there." He smacked one fist into the other palm. "An ambush for an ambush."

"Yes, sir!" Pyle bent to his task, and Demming nodded. The move would give them a little more time to prepare, and if all went well they'd gain the element of surprise. If not, well, they'd have a little extra cover from the rocks they would be hiding within. That was still something.

And right now he'd take any advantage he could get.

# CHAPTER TWENTY-ONE

"STRAP IN TIGHT," LIZETTE WARNED, her hands tightening on the wheel. "This could get bumpy." She was back at her customary place at the helm, preparing to guide the *Remora* into the fast-moving jumble of rocks directly ahead. Pyle had been only too glad to relinquish control to her in the face of those stone slivers, not that Demming could blame him. Maneuvering the ship into those tight quarters, and at full speed, was work for a master.

Fortunately, Lizette had been one of the finest natural pilots the Royal Navy had seen in years. And their journey thus far had only honed her skill.

Even so, Demming checked to make sure the webbing on his command chair was locked in securely. All around him, his officers did the same. None of them wanted to miss this.

They approached the first rock in a rush, its sharp, uneven edges expanding rapidly in their front canopy, but Lizette stood calmly in her place. She tugged the wheel gently, and the *Remora*'s nose angled down and to one side, tilting the ship so it slid past that jagged front and entered the loose stone forest in earnest. At the same time, she raised the throttle, easing off on the engines so the *Remora*'s speed lessened slightly. Then she fired the jets, slowing the ship further. She couldn't cut their motion completely, however, or the rocks would tear the ship apart as they hurtled past. She had to match the cluster's speed, and trajectory, while finding them a spot far enough within that they were shielded from view. Not an easy task, but Demming couldn't think of anyone he'd rather have making the attempt.

The next few minutes were tense. He couldn't help gripping his chair's armrests and leaning this way and that as Lizette danced the *Remora* among the rocks. He suspected he hadn't taken a proper breath since they'd entered the cluster, just short little gasps as an edge loomed alongside them or a peak suddenly swam into view. It was like riding a strong current through a coral reef, trying to navigate the twisty openings at full speed, knowing the coral could shred skin and suit alike if you even brushed against it.

But Lizette had phenomenal control of their ship. She tilted it up and down, angled it left and right, swept it over and under, even shimmied it sideways once when one rock struck another and suddenly spun the second on its axis, razor-sharp tips pivoting toward their hull.

At last, however, she sighed and removed one hand from the wheel long enough to flex her fingers, before returning that hand to its place and repeating the process with her other. "We're here," she announced over her shoulder, never taking her eyes from the canopy or from her monitors and scopes. "This is right near the heart of the cluster, and we've got enough room around us that we should be safe from the rocks as long as we maintain their pace, but the *Siren Knife* shouldn't be able to detect us here—we should just show up as another rock. Plus I've got a clear exit—up over this one stone in front of us, a slight twist to the right, and we can punch the engines and zoom right through to clear ether." The pride and relief were evident in her voice, and Demming smiled. She'd certainly earned both.

"Well done, Miss Mills," he congratulated her, and noticed the way she straightened slightly. "That was an amazing piece of piloting." He let her bask in the compliment a moment before hitting the speaking tube. "Miss Cuny, we should be within range of the *Siren Knife* in two hours. I want you to target them, engines and weapons, as soon as you can, but don't fire. Keep an eye on their weapons. If they go hot, hit them with everything you've got. If they don't, hold your fire until we're on top of them—I want to be able to close the second we've incapacitated them."

"Yes, sir!" He knew she was itching to shoot, but he also knew she'd follow his orders precisely. Molly Cuny was no fool—she knew they might not be able to disable the pirate ship on the first volley, and if that was true they were better off being close in, where the other vessel might not have room to maneuver or to aim effectively.

Even so, they were taking a major risk. They just didn't know enough about the pirates' capabilities. How much damage could their ship's armor withstand? How heavily shielded were their engines? How powerful were their weapons? How many times could they fire, and how long did it take them to recharge? Did the ship have any weak spots? If he could find an unprotected area he could hit that and take out the crew directly, before they could fight back. It wasn't the most honorable approach, but in a fight for survival, against experienced foes, Demming was willing to use any means necessary. These were the men who had killed his captain and stolen their water, after all. He did not intend to show them any mercy.

The thought of their theft sparked something in him. A thought began to form, something about the seal when the *Siren*

*Knife*'s crew had boarded them—

He had it.

In an instant he was unfastening his webbing and rising, half-flinging himself from his chair. "I'll be right back," he explained as Dittmer and Pasic and Pyle looked up, questions clear on their faces. "I just need to check on something." Lizette didn't even glance back at him as he made his way to the door. Which was fine—she needed to concentrate on the rocks.

He needed to confirm a suspicion. And if he was right, he might have a way for them to turn the tables on the pirate ship. An ironically fitting way, at that.

"I think it will work," Amelia agreed after he'd explained it to her, the pieces falling into place as he spoke. That was why he'd wanted to speak to her in person, rather than through the speaking tube. This way he was able to bounce the idea off her, and thrash it out as he went. With the speaking tube he felt as if he could ask short, simple questions and issue orders but not much more—it was an excellent tool but it didn't accommodate a full exchange of ideas.

Besides, it was an excuse to see her, and Demming wasn't above using it.

"It's terrible," she continued, shuddering slightly. "If you're right—it's an awful way to go about it. You know that." She shook her head, and her mouth firmed into a narrow line. "Still, it's no more than they deserve."

"Exactly." Demming wasn't happy about the idea himself, but if it meant the difference between their survival and their death, he'd take it. "I need to know where, though. As precisely as you can."

"That shouldn't be a problem, actually." She favored

him with a small smile. "I know when they boarded us they couldn't see through our panels and doors, which is why they didn't know about our personal weapons, or about the food in the galley. We don't have that problem. I can get clear readings on their ship's interior—not enough to paint you a picture, perhaps, but enough to draw a map. And our systems can register differences in pressure and density." Her smile broadened. "I can tell you precisely where it is, and from there it'll be easy to figure out an access point."

"Good. Let Miss Cuny know the second you have that location." He turned to go. "Thanks."

"My pleasure, sir." There was mockery in her voice, but only a little, and it was light and teasing. Then she turned serious again. "Good luck."

He nodded. Even with this, they were going to need it.

"We're coming up on them, sir," Lizette reported a little over two hours later. "We'll cross their path in ten minutes, provided we don't speed up."

Demming nodded. He was back in his chair, and he leaned back, one hand propping up his chin as he thought it through. Everything was in place. They were as ready as they'd ever be. "No sign that they've spotted us?"

"No, sir." It was Pyle who answered. "Their weapons are still idle, they haven't changed course or speed, and they haven't scanned us as far as we can tell."

"All right." Demming took a deep breath. "Miss Cuny?"

"Target locked and weapons ready, sir," she reported crisply through the speaking tube.

"Excellent. Miss Mills, prepare to take us out of these rocks—I want us on top of the *Siren Knife* the minute we fire."

He waited just long to see her nod. "Miss Cuny, fire at will."

"Yes, sir!"

The ship rocked a second later, and continued to vibrate as Lizette immediately spun the wheel and lowed the throttle. The *Remora* leaped forward, clearing the rock before it like a startled fish, and the engines thrummed to life as she fed them more power.

Demming kept his eyes locked ahead, watching the *Siren Knife* through the gaps in the stones. He saw the ship shudder as the first blast struck, targeting the very tips of its side-mounted gun turrets. Molly Cuny followed immediately with a second volley, striking the pirate vessel's forward guns and then its engines. Finally she struck with a third attack, this time hitting a spot two-thirds of the way back—she had saved their newest guns for this volley, and had narrowed their focus to a tight, sharp point, strong enough to cut through even heavy armor plating but not large enough to cause much damage.

Unless you knew exactly where to apply it.

"Side guns destroyed," she reported gleefully, even as Lizette swiveled the ship clear of the cluster and brought it around toward the pirates. "Forward guns inoperable. Engines damaged—they might be functional, but only for a crawl."

Demming waited, holding his breath and clenching his jaw.

"Hull pierced," the tiny gunner's mate continued after a moment. "I can't be sure—"

"I can," Amelia cut in—of course she'd been listening to the conversation. "The entire interior density just changed in a hurry. I'd say it was a direct hit." Her voice was flat, and Demming knew she was warring with the same feelings that were wrestling within him—satisfaction and guilt.

"Bring us alongside them, Miss Mills," he told his pilot. "And line up our forward seal with their lock. Mister Kesselman?"

"Aye, captain?" The bo'sun answered through the speaking tube.

"Ready a full boarding party. Most of the pirates should be incapacitated, but there may be a few who acted quickly enough to survive. Issue full weapons and warn the men—this kill or be killed."

"Yes, sir!" Kesselman sounded almost as eager as Molly Cuny had, and Demming knew the powerful boatswain was looking forward to getting revenge for Captain Mendez's death. So were most of the crew. He'd have no shortage of volunteers for the boarding party.

For a moment Demming was tempted to go with them. But he doubted his officers would let him get away with putting himself at risk a second time.

"Sir?" That was Pyle, cautiously raising a hand. "Can I ask, sir—what exactly did we just do to them?" Some of the others nodded. Demming hadn't explained his plan, just in case it hadn't worked. Now, however, he favored them with a slow, satisfied grin.

"We targeted their holding tanks," he answered. "Specifically, the seals where those holding tanks connected to the rest of the interior." He pounded one fist on his arm rest. "They stole our water—so we flooded them with it."

That was what had come to him earlier, while thinking about their previous encounter. He remembered that the *Siren Knife* had deliberately kept its pressure less than theirs when attempting a seal, so any danger in the atmosphere would stay on the *Remora* and not rise through the seal. His first thought had been something about reversing the pressure difference and flooding the pirate ship with poison gas. But they didn't even have any poison, and the pirates would never let them get that close.

But then his brain had latched onto the word "flooding." And he'd remembered that the pirates had their water.

Enough water to fill the entire *Remora*.

And the *Siren Knife* was roughly the same size.

But Demming and the rest of the *Remora*'s crew could breathe underwater.

The pirates couldn't.

He'd conferred with Amelia, who'd agreed—if they could locate and target the holding tanks right where at their seals, they could send all that water crashing through the *Siren Knife* in an instant. They could drown the pirates in seconds.

Theoretically, they could take the entire pirate ship without a fight.

Demming knew better than to expect that, however. If the flood had drowned half of the pirates, and thrown the rest off-balance, that would be enough.

"Boarding party ready, sir," Kesselman reported through the speaking tube. Demming ground his teeth. He really wanted to go with them!

But he knew he couldn't. Instead he did the next best thing. "Mister Pyle!" The young officer snapped to attention. "Arm yourself and meet Mister Kesselman at the forward lock. You're my eyes and ears."

"Yes, sir!" Pyle practically sprinted to the foredeck door, and was through it before it had finished cycling open. Demming wished he could join him.

"Manuevering over the lock," Lizette announced, and Demming snapped his gaze back to the front. They had cleared the rest of the rocks, which were now speeding past and away, and were literally on top of the *Siren Knife*. It had put up no resistance, which meant either they'd killed the ship's defenses—or they'd killed the entire pirate crew.

Or both.

Either way, he wasn't taking any chances. "Mister Kesselman, stand ready," he ordered. "You'll go through as soon as the seal is in place. Be careful."

"Yes, sir."

Demming watched as the *Remora* slid closer and closer to the *Siren Knife*, until—with the faintest shudder—the two ships brushed up against each other, ever so gently. Like two fish kissing as they swam past.

"Activating the seal," Amelia reported from engineering, and Demming was glad she was still back there, well away from the action. He didn't expect it to spill into the *Remora*, but if it did he wanted her someplace safe. "Equalizing pressure—"

"Keep ours a little less than theirs," Demming cut in. "Just like they did. We don't want any surprises leaking through."

"Of course. Adjusting pressure. The lock is secure."

"Mister Kesselman, Mister Pyle, you are clear to board the pirate ship," Demming informed them. "Set someone by the lock to keep it secure, and report back once you've swept the other vessel."

"Yes, sir!" Even through the speaking tube he thought he could hear the crewmen rustling about as they gripped weapons and stood in formation behind Kesselman and Pyle. Then, with a distant clang, the *Remora*'s forward lock slid open, and Demming knew his men were making their way onto the pirate ship.

He hoped they didn't find any unpleasant surprises.

# CHAPTER TWENTY-TWO

Ten minutes passed. Then twenty. Demming fretted in his chair, then rose to pace the length of the foredeck, hands behind his back. It was taking too long. He should have heard something by now. He stared out the window at the *Siren Knife*'s prow, just visible above them. What was going on in there? Were his men all right? Had they encountered opposition? What was keeping them from reporting back?

When the speaking-tube squawked, he turned and practically dove at the chair, grabbing the tube and slamming his palm flat on the activation button. "Demming here—report!"

"Captain!" It was a crewman, Demming knew he'd seen the man but couldn't quite remember his name—Ford, perhaps? "There's movement on the other side of the seal!" Ah, so this was one of the men Kesselman had set to guard the lock. "Someone's coming through! They're—"

He heard a hauntingly familiar sound, a soft whump like a drawn-out gasp for air. Then a heavier thump, which he knew with bone-chilling certainty was the noise of a body hitting the floor.

Then the speaking-tube went dead.

"Intruders!" Demming bellowed, straightening and slapping

his hands to the inside walls of the chair's armrests. Each of the chairs here had built-in compartments to hold essentials secure during maneuvers. Captain Mendez had kept a book and a small journal in them, along with a picture of her family and a length of seaweed she'd been braiding into some shape. Demming had removed those after the *Houndstooth* encounter, placing them with the rest of his late captain's effects and replacing them with objects he hoped he would never need—

—the saw-toothed blade he'd taken off the one smuggler, and a pistol he'd gleaned from the pile of their confiscated weapons.

Now he hefted one in each hand and charged for the door.

Suddenly there was a figure in his path. A tall, slender figure. "Captain—"

"Not now, doctor," Demming warned through gritted teeth. "They've breached our ship! Sound the alarm and get out of my way!"

They locked gazes for an instant. Then Pasic nodded and stepped aside. "Be careful," was all he added as Demming shoved past, hit the door button, and ran through it once there was enough space to squeeze by.

The foredeck was located just front of the ship's center. The forward lock was a little ways in front of that, near the *Remora*'s nose, but it was a straight shot and Demming took it at full speed. He'd gone maybe twenty paces when the ship's alarm sounded. He'd all but reached the forward compartment when crewmen emerged from the crew quarters right beside it.

"Stand back!" he warned as he approached. "We've got pirates in there!" He noted with approval that the men were armed and ready. "Be prepared to fire the minute you have a shot!" Various nods responded, and he hit the door control and then pivoted back to the side, ready to peek through and shoot.

The door irised slowly, or so it seemed to him. As the panels parted he caught glimpses of the forward compartment beyond: hull walls; textured floor; sloping ceiling with the open lock inset; something large and pale on the floor, splayed and unmoving; figures shifting to the side, weapons raised—

There!

He aimed and fired, and was pleased to see one of the suited figures stumble. A second shot hit the same pirate, aimed by one of the crewmen behind him, and Demming watched the intruder spin about and topple. He was already sighting on the next invader, however.

The door was completely open now, and Demming could see clearly. There were at least three other pirates in the compartment, all crouched behind equipment lockers they had tugged away from the walls, and he could make out Ford and two other crewmen dead on the floor. He could make out steam rising from their fallen forms.

That meant Suwa Jem and his marauders had now killed five of the *Remora*'s crew. Assuming Kesselman, Pyle, and the rest of the boarding party were still alive.

Demming growled and ground his teeth. He would not let them butcher any more of his men.

He traded shots with one of the pirates, but knew he had little chance of hitting anything while they had such solid cover. He had to get in there, or get the pirates to come out. But how?

And he had to do it fast, in case they were preparing to send more men through from the *Siren Knife*. Enough pirates and they could overpower him and the crewmen and take the *Remora*.

He couldn't let that happen.

He glanced around, looking for anything that could help. But the only things he saw were the pirates, his crew, Ford and the other dead men, the equipment lockers, and the lock itself. Nothing.

Unless—

He thought quickly. The gun he was using wasn't one of their sonic pistols, it was on the *Houndstooth*'s weapons. It generated some kind of energy blast, far more concussive and explosive than their own guns. Messier, and more aggressive.

And more destructive to solid objects.

Demming aimed carefully—directly at the nearest equipment locker. Then he pulled the trigger. And held it down.

His gun bucked in his hands, and gouts of light and heat shot from it. Centered on one spot on the locker.

With a loud burst, the metal locker door shattered, shards flying.

He kept firing at the same spot.

And, a second later, a second explosion signaled the destruction of the locker's rear wall.

The pirate crouched behind it screamed and lurched to his feet, staggering about as he clutched at the shrapnel imbedded in his chest and limbs.

Demming shot him in the head, and the intruder's screams ended at once as his body dropped.

One down.

At least two to go.

Something else occurred to him. "Fetch me a ball," he ordered one of the crew closest to him. "Actually, bring as many as you can."

The crewmember, a tall woman with dark hair pulled back tight, stared at him for a second, then grinned. "Yes, sir!" She ducked back around the others and vanished into the crew quarters.

She returned a minute later with three large, heavy balls. The crew used them for various games like football and basketball.

They were perfect.

Demming sheathed his knife and took one, hefting it. It was good and solid. The crewmember had already passed the second ball to one of the others, and she had the third in her own hands. He met her gaze, and then that of her companion, and nodded.

"On three," he whispered.

"One."

"Two."

"Three!"

And he lobbed the ball as hard as he could—

—past the equipment lockers, past the pirates, and into the forward compartment.

Right against the rear wall.

Both pirates targeted the balls as they flew past, but their shots did little to slow the heavy spheres. Then the balls struck the rear walls and rebounded—

—right into the pirates themselves.

One pirate lost his footing and half-rose as the ball jostled him to the side. A pair of sonic bursts took him in the chest and shoulder the second he was clear, and another caught him in the head even as he toppled.

The other pirate grunted in what sounded like pain. Then Demming heard a clatter.

He waited a second. Nothing, just the gentle thud of the balls as their bouncing slowed and finally stopped.

It was quiet.

"I think we knocked him out," he told the crew. "But be wary. They're full of tricks."

He led the way between the lockers, pistol in hand, redrawing the knife as he went.

But as he rounded the third locker he saw the pirate stretched out, unmoving.

One of the heavy balls lay beside its helmeted head.

They had evidently scored a direct hit.

Demming didn't waste any time. He aimed at the pirate's chest and fired. The body jerked once, then flopped back down.

Now he knew the pirate wasn't faking.

A quick scan of the room confirmed that it was clear again.

"You and you," Demming said, gesturing at the woman and man who'd helped with the balls. "Grab their guns and come with me. The rest of you, guard this room. No more pirates will set foot on the *Remora*. Clear?" They all nodded.

He barely waited long enough for the two to arm themselves before leading them through the seal and into the *Siren Knife*.

The second they stepped through, water surrounded them. Demming allowed himself half a second to breathe it in, closing his mouth and expanding his gills, luxuriating in the feel of being immersed once more. Waves, that felt good! He could feel new energy coursing through him as his body pulled oxygen from the water as well. So much more efficient than mouth-breathing!

He was here on a mission, however, and couldn't let himself get distracted. He signaled the two crewmembers to stay close, and swam farther into the pirate ship.

There was a bend in the corridor up ahead, and he rounded it—to find a body floating right in front of him, brushing gently against the ceiling.

Three arms dangled in the water. Three legs drifted behind. The pirate didn't have a helmet on, and Demming could see one of that race's face clearly for the first time. Its eyes—there were three, as he'd once guessed, ranged evenly around beneath a heavy brow—were wide and staring, and its beaked mouth that resembled a squid's hung slack.

It had drowned.

Demming pushed it aside and continued past, ignoring the short pang of guilt. They had deserved this, for what they'd done to Captain Mendez and Mister Carruthers and who knew how many others.

That didn't change the fact that he had killed them.

But he hoped it would help him live with it.

In order to do that, however, he would have to live. And that meant eliminating any pirates who had survived the sudden deluge.

After turning another corner and finding himself in a wider corridor that he suspected ran the length of the ship, Demming paused. And listened.

Water was an excellent conductor. And he could hear faint noises coming from up ahead.

Sounds—like gunfire.

He quickened his pace.

The *Siren Knife*'s control cabin seemed to be at the very prow, taking up the space right behind those nasty pincer-like prongs and guns, and the sounds seemed to be emanating from there. Demming was sure he felt the familiar vibration of sonic pistols, and the other was the whump of the pirates' weapons.

He swam as fast as he could, pistol out before him.

He hoped it was waterproof.

The front cabin had sturdy doors but they were open, and he

glided quickly past them, pulling his legs up and then kicking out to angle to the side as soon as he had.

Which proved to be a good thing, since it got him out of the middle of the firefight occurring there.

"Captain?" Pyle asked as Demming swam up beside him and then dropped down behind what seemed to be an overturned stool or chair. "What are you doing here?"

"We got worried," Demming replied, shooting at a pirate on the far side of the room. "And then they sent a handful of brigands through the seal." He nodded at the younger officer's expression. "We took care of them. But I thought you might need a hand."

"You just wanted in on the action, you mean," Kesselman replied from behind a nearby table, but the bo'sun smiled as he said it. "Well, much obliged, sir. We cleared out the rest with no problem—most of them were dead already, from the water—but the ones in here were better prepared, I guess. They're all suited up, and they've got plenty of cover. It's sort of a waiting game, really. Sooner or later one side's going to make a mistake."

"Let's just hope it's not us," one of the boarding party muttered, firing over the table from his spot beside the boatswain. Demming nodded. The pirates knew this ship far better than they did. They had the advantage here. And in their suits, they didn't have to worry about the water.

But how long could they survive in those suits, he wondered?

He didn't want to have to find out.

"We need something to get them out in the open," he muttered.

But what?

Would the same tricks they'd used in the *Remora* work here?

Balls wouldn't bounce as well, or hit as hard, underwater.

And the stools and tables were thicker than their equipment lockers. He wasn't sure he could shoot through them.

He glanced around. This control cabin was very different from his own. It was blockier, like the rest of the ship. Everything on the *Remora* was smooth curves and gentle sweeps— everything here was sharp edges and harsh angles. Even the lighting was different—some kind of glowing tubes that hung suspended at intervals along the ceiling, now sparking in places where the water was seeping into their wiring.

Which might be the answer to their problem.

First Demming glanced over him and his crew. Yes, there were similar fixtures above them. They'd have to be quick, before the pirates caught on and tried the same thing.

"Aim for the lights," he whispered to Pyle. "Pass the word."

His midshipman nodded and shared the information quietly with the man on his other side.

After a minute, everyone looked ready. They all watched Demming for a signal.

He took a breath, again savoring the feeling of water entering his gills, and nodded.

Then he raised his pistol and fired.

His first shot was a complete miss, striking a panel on the wall.

The second, however, caught a fixture right on its end. The concussive burst shattered the link there, and the light swung down in a glittering, sparking arc—

—right into one of the pirates crouched on that side of the cabin.

The pirate jerked upright reflexively when the light crashed into him, whirling about to see what new attack this was—

—and Pyle caught him in the conical helmet, the sonic burst

slamming the stocky figure into the wall. The pirate collapsed and didn't move again.

The rest of the crew had targeted the lights as well, and within second all of the fixtures on that side were swinging free or outright dropping. The tactic threw the pirates into confusion. One apparently died from electrocution, a light fixture's trailing wires touching a metal plate on his suit and sending a vicious charge surging through him. Two others fell from sonic fire as they rose to avoid the falling lights. One actually got shot by his own fellow when a light struck the second one's arm and knocked his pistol to the side just as he fired.

There were two left, however. One was built even more oddly than the others, from what little Demming could see around the stools and tables and bodies—it had four flailing limbs up top, and many more below, almost like an octopus had somehow been poured into one of the pirates' suits.

The other Demming recognized instantly.

Suwa Jem.

He felt anger course through him at the sight of the pirate captain, and had a sudden flash of Captain Mendez laying on the *Remora*'s puddled floor, eyes squeezed shut, skin drained of color.

Her murderer was on the other side of this room.

Demming didn't even think about it. He just kicked upward and dove across the gap, firing the entire way.

"Captain!" After a second's surprise, Pyle began firing as well, covering him. Kesselman and the others joined suit. The strange pirate apparently decided this would be a good time to run, and launched itself upward as well, its tentacles flailing. A dozen sonic bursts took it before it had fully cleared its cover.

Which just left Suwa Jem himself.

The pirate captain rose to his feet as Demming approached, all three legs solidly planted. It raised its own pistol—that same long, bulky, ugly weapon that had killed Mendez—and aimed it slowly, almost casually at Demming. It seemed Suwa Jem was not afraid to die, provided he could take Demming with him.

But the pirate clearly hadn't realized how fast Royal Navy men could swim. Or how much water could slow simple movement. Demming was on him before the pistol's barrel had fully swung around, and swept downward with his off hand—

—the one holding the saw-toothed blade.

The sharp, jagged edge sliced into the pirate captain's arm, shearing through his armored suit and the flesh beneath, and Suwa Jem gasped, jerking his injured limb back. The pistol fell slowly to the floor.

Demming arced down and scooped it up, then flipped over, adjusting his grip on the strange weapon as his head came up.

By the time he was level with Suwa Jem, the pirate captain had his own gun pointed at his chest.

Demming thought he could see eyes widen through the conical helmet.

"This is for Captain Mendez," he whispered.

Then he pulled the trigger.

That same soft *whump* sent a shiver up his arm, and Suwa Jem jerked once, than crumpled.

Demming shot him again in the head, just to be sure.

"It's over," he told his men as they swam over to cluster protectively around him. He nudged the pirate captain's body with one foot.

"We've won."

# CHAPTER TWENTY-THREE

"THIS SHIP IS ASTOUNDING." AMELIA shook her head. "It'll take me a while to figure all of it out. They appear to have taken bits and pieces from other ships and just cobbled them all together. I doubt the *Siren Knife* looks anything like its original shape, whatever that was."

"Not a bad trick," Dittmer pointed out. Demming had sent Pyle back to take charge of the *Remora* and summoned his quartermaster and engineer instead. The three of them were walking the *Siren Knife*, examining the pirate vessel they had now captured. Kesselman and his men were still combing the ship ahead of them, making sure there weren't any other survivors or nasty surprises.

"If there's anything like a Royal Navy out here, or even just a wave patrol," the heavy-set quartermaster continued, "they'd most likely have records of all the standard ship types—and their weaknesses." He rapped a knuckle on the *Siren Knife*'s corridor wall, producing a hollow echo. "This ship is unique, so they wouldn't know where to hit it right away."

"Plus this way they can trade out parts every time they find something better," Demming mused. "Faster engines, bigger guns, stronger shielding."

"We've already started doing something similar ourselves," Amelia pointed out. "We've just managed to integrate our new components more smoothly. They clearly cared more for function than for appearance."

And why not, Demming thought. They were pirates, after all. They didn't have to look pretty, or even clean. And out here in the ether there was no need for streamlining—they could build on pieces all they liked and not lose any speed because of it.

"Can we use some of it ourselves?" he asked, and Amelia frowned.

"We could," she answered after a moment. "But it would be tricky. Our engines are better, I think, though theirs aren't far off. They have better weaponry and better armor, but we'd have to tie those into our systems somehow, and I'm not sure the *Remora*—"

"Captain!" A crewwoman came racing down the corridor. "There's something here Mister Kesselman says you need to see!"

"Lead the way." Demming kicked off from the floor at once, and Amelia and Dittmer fell in beside him as they swam after the woman. Once again he luxuriated in the feel of being back in the water. How had he managed to survive so long in nothing but air?

The woman led them down the corridor to around its midpoint. There was a hatch in the ceiling, and she flip-kicked upward, gliding smoothly through the circular opening. Demming followed suit. Clearly Kesselman's crew had already inspected whatever lay beyond, so he doubted there was any danger. But then what could be so urgent?

He found out as he entered the small room. Consoles lined

the walls, monitors above them or inset within them. Judging by the targeting sights on each monitor, they were linked to the pirate ship's weapons. This was its gunnery.

But what caught his attention was less the controls and more the creature cowering among them.

Demming had been stunned but fascinated at the first glimpse of whatever the pirates had been. He had been amazed at the researchers, and intrigued by the bestial smugglers. This new sight was every bit as bewildering as any of those.

The creature seemed to be of average size—at least, the two crewmen Kellerman had flanking it were neither dwarfed nor made to seem gigantic. It had some sort of segmented belt around its middle, and a visor of some type covered its large eyes.

The rest of it was bare, however. Which gave Demming and the others a clear view of its eight wriggling limbs, its large, round head, and its small, beaked mouth.

"An octopus." Demming looked over at Kesselman, but his bo'sun merely shrugged. "Why would the pirates have an octopus? And why keep it in here?"

He was surprised but not completely shocked when the creature opened its mouth and answered. "I am not an octopus, whatever that may be," it replied. Its voice was thin, high, and wavery. "I am a Lacmupo. Are you pirates, come to claim this ship as your own, or has justice finally caught up with the butchers of the *Siren Knife*?"

"We are members of Her Majesty's Royal Navy," Demming replied. "I am Nate Demming, captain of the HMES *Remora*. Are you saying you were a captive of some sort?"

"Indeed I was," the creature—it still looked like an octopus to him—said. It waved its tentacles about. "My name is Mirsux.

I was part of the explorer ship Depth of Knowledge. We were traversing space, seeking knowledge, when the *Siren Knife* found us. They damaged our ship, killed my friends, and then made off with our supplies, our money, and whatever parts of the ship they fancied." It writhed in agitation. "For some reason they decided I might be useful to them, so they carried me off as well. Then I was given a choice—help them with their weapons or be eaten."

"Well, you're safe now," Demming promised the shivering creature. "We'll get you back home somehow, or wherever else it is you want to go." He ignored the sharp glance Amelia was giving him. "Though we are on a mission, so I hope you aren't in a hurry."

"Not at all," the strange Lacmupo replied. "I am just happy to be rid of them. They were truly the worst of the worst."

"Demming nodded. "How long were you forced to aid them?"

"Over six months," Mirsux answered. "And I dreaded each and every day of it." It hung its large head. "Yet I also feared the day they had no further need of me, and killed me as well."

"Nothing wrong with that," Demming assured the strange creature. "We all want to live, if we can." He patted Dittmer on the arm. "This is Mister Dittmer, my quartermaster. If you've been on this ship for six months, you must know it fairly well. I'd like you to help him tally things up—show him where everything's kept, including any compartments we might not have found."

The octopoid stranger nodded. "Certainly. It is the least I can do as thanks for your gaining me my freedom, and avenging my friends."

"And what about you?" Amelia asked as Dittmer and the

tentacled Mirsux floated off together. "What are you going to do?"

"I need to think about a few things," Demming replied. "It's time we figure out exactly what to do next, and how."

A few hours later, he called a meeting in the officers' mess. Only Craddick wasn't present, as he was manning the *Remora's* foredeck. Demming didn't expect trouble, but he'd learned not to let his guard down.

"We've studied the ship," Amelia reported. "We could use some of their materials but, as I've already mentioned, it would be difficult to synch those components with our own system."

"What if we didn't?" Demming asked her. "What if we left their pieces on their ship, and kept ours on the *Remora*?"

"So we just leave it there?" Lizette asked. "That seems like a waste."

"We aren't going to leave anything," he told her. "We're taking the entire ship with us. We're just keeping it intact." He smiled. "And letting the *Remora* live up to her name."

"But how—" He saw Amelia's eyes widen as she got it. "Of course! We attach the *Remora* to the *Siren Knife* much as she is now, only with the rear seal so the two are more closely aligned. When we fire up the *Siren Knife's* engines she'll drag the *Remora* along, and vice-versa. Fire both at once and we could double, maybe even triple, our normal speed."

"We wouldn't have any better armor," Pyle pointed out. Then he grinned. "Though I suppose we'd have an entire ship to use as a shield, if it came to that."

"Exactly." Demming paced along the table. "By linking the two we can take advantage of the *Siren Knife's* systems. And if anything goes wrong we can just close the lock, sever the bond, and push off."

"We can't fill both ships with water," Dittmer pointed out. "They didn't have much beyond what they stole from us, and it isn't like we've found any more."

"Bring all the water back onto the *Remora*," Demming ordered. "And reset the pressure on the *Siren Knife* so the water stays on our side of things. We'll rotate a skeleton crew through there, just enough to keep it synched with us. Maybe we can find a way to slave its navigation systems to our own"—he looked at Lizette and Amelia, and both nodded—"but we'll still want someone there to keep an eye on things." He frowned. "Which brings us to the next question—what to do with our unexpected guest."

"He doesn't want to go home," Amelia stated. She shrugged when the others turned to stare at her. "We got to talking while looking over the *Siren Knife*'s engines. He was sent out to explore, and he still wants to do that. He just didn't want to be enslaved in the process."

"Are we sure he was really a captive, and not just another pirate looking to save his own skin?" Kesselman asked.

"He seems sincere," Dittmer offered. "I think he really was dragooned into service."

"I agree," Amelia chimed in. She and Dittmer had spent the most time with the Lacmupo thus far. "I think he's a decent man—fish—I mean person—and he certainly knows that ship far better than we do."

"He's also amphibious, like us," Lizette pointed out. "That's how he survived, right? Which means he could handle a sudden flooding, like the one we used on the pirates today. That's probably important."

Demming rubbed a hand over his head. It would definitely be useful to have someone on board who knew the other ship, and who could handle the air-to-water transition if necessary.

"All right," he decided. "We'll let Mirsux to join our crew, at least on a probationary basis. He can retain control of the *Siren Knife*'s gunnery. We'll send Molly Cuny over to confer with him."

He sighed and stopped walking, leaning forward with both fists on the table. "I want to talk about something else as well," he explained to his assembled officers. "I've been thinking about what the researchers told me. The *Remora* is a handsome target, and we'll draw a lot of attacks as we travel. Unless we do something about it." He straightened and crossed his arms. "And I know just the thing to do it."

"The best way not to be constant prey—is to become a predator ourselves."

"What do you mean?" Pasic asked softly, but Demming suspected by the way the doctor's eyes had narrowed that he already suspected the answer. A few others were shaking their heads as well, but Demming continued on.

"We need to become pirates."

The conference room erupted as everyone started to talk at once. Demming let them argue and exclaim for a moment. Then he slammed a fist on the table. That got their attention, and the noise fell away.

"Thank you. Now then, I've given this a lot of thought. With our new weaponry, we can put up a decent fight against most attackers, I think. But that still means having to fight our way past every smuggler or pirate that sees us. And the Researchers warned that there were a lot of them." He glared at his officers. "Isn't it better if most of them run when they see us, instead?"

"Certainly," Amelia agreed. "But that doesn't mean—"

"They don't know anything about the Royal Navy out here

in the ether," Demming stated, cutting her off. He felt bad about that, but he'd known all along that she and Pasic would be the two hardest to convince. He had to stop her from making a strong argument against his proposal. "They won't recognize our authority. They do understand force, though. And violence. If word gets around to steer clear of us, most of them will respect that."

"So you're saying we just pretend we're pirates, then?" Pyle asked.

But Demming shook his head. "No. That would never work—it would just be a story, with no proof. To show we're a real threat, we have to become pirates. We have to attack and raid other ships. At least a few, until news of us spreads." He grinned. "But we can be selective in our targets."

"Like the *Houndstooth*," Kesselman offered. "Those rotten scoundrels deserved what they got."

"Exactly like them," Demming agreed. "Smugglers and other pirates, whenever possible." He sighed. "We would have to hit at least one or two science vessels or passenger ships, though, if we wanted our new identity to be convincing. We could be careful, however—we'd only do temporary damage, and we'd leave them with enough food and water and fuel to limp to a safe harbor afterward. No killing except in self-defense, no taking prisoners, no taking liberties with others— we're still Royal Navy, no matter what we may pretend." He met each officer's gaze in turn. "I know it seems a slippery slope, but I think we can maintain the cover and still hold true to our values, our training, and our mission."

He gave them time to mull that over.

"I like it," Lizette stated, the first to break the silence. "It gives us freedom to move around, keeps most other ships from trying us, and lets us take out those we'd normally pursue and punish anyway." She nodded. "Count me in."

Pyle nodded as well. "As long as we're just doing this to avoid conflict, and not really going rogue, I'm for it," the young officer agreed.

"You've got me on board," Kesselman offered. Dittmer nodded. Both men were pragmatists, Demming knew, and recognized this as being their best chance to survive the ether.

He'd included Quentin and Molly Cuny in this meeting, and they both agreed to the plan as well. "Pirate galleys are a little more relaxed anyway," Quentin joked. "Guess this means I can break out a few of my less conventional recipes now." Molly Cuny didn't say a word, but she nodded.

That only left Amelia and Doctor Pasic.

"I don't like it," Pasic admitted. "It seems a dangerous path to start upon." He sighed. "But it would keep the *Remora* and her crew safe, and that is my top priority."

"I give you full permission to call me on it any time you think I'm crossing the line," Demming assured the doctor. "You're the ship's conscience already. Now you can be mine as well." He grinned, and after a moment Pasic smiled back.

Amelia still seemed unconvinced, however.

"Trust me on this," Demming told her softly, stepping up beside her and taking her hands in his. "I will do as little damage as possible to the innocent ships we board, and I will do my best to keep all of us out of harm's way. But this really is the best way to discourage attack."

"I know it is," she agreed quietly, squeezing his hands. "I just—I hate the idea of anyone running in fear of us. Not brigands and the like—they should run. But innocents. I hate that."

"So do I," Demming admitted. "But it can't be avoided. Still, if they run from us, that means they'll stay safe. Much as I'd love to stop and meet every ship we cross, that would not only be dangerous, it would slow our mission to a crawl. This is for the best."

She nodded slowly, just a mild incline of her chin, then again more strongly. "All right. Yes. But don't expect me to keep quiet if you start behaving like a pirate in truth."

"Fair enough." He didn't want to release her hands, but he knew he had to. For now, at least. So he clasped them a second more, then stepped back.

"It's official, then," he announced. "As of this moment, we are no longer the HMES *Remora*. We are now the *Dread Remora*, pirate ship and marauder. The *Siren Knife* will help promote that new image, and once we've targeted a few other ships the rest of the ether will get the message."

Everyone nodded, and slowly they dispersed. Demming leaned back against the table. This was what had come to him earlier, and he was half relieved and half dismayed that the notion had now become a reality. He was a pirate captain!

Still, it was for the good of their mission. And he would do his best to maintain the discipline and honor of the Royal Navy, even while he spread fear of his name throughout the ether.

As he rose and walked from the room, heading toward the foredeck, Demming admitted that none of this was what he had expected.

But he also couldn't deny the fact that he was having the time of his life.

# ACKNOWLEDGMENTS

THIS BOOK WOULDN'T HAVE BEEN possible without my partners in crime, Dave and Steve. Cheers, guys!

I also want to thank those friends who took the time to read chapters while I was working on the book, and when I put them up on Crossroad's blog. The feedback and the encouragement helped a great deal.

Thanks as always to my lovely wife and our wonderful children, who inspire and motivate me every day.

Finally, thank you those of you who decided to buy this book and accompany me on this journey. I hope you've enjoyed the first appearance of the *Dread Remora*—rest assured, Nate Demming and his crew have many more adventures ahead of them!

# ABOUT THE AUTHOR

AARON ROSENBERG IS AN AWARD-WINNING, #1 bestselling novelist, children's book author, and game designer. His novels include the best-selling DuckBob series (consisting of *No Small Bills*, *Too Small for Tall*, and the forthcoming *Three Small Coinkydinks*), the *Dread Remora* space-opera series and, with David Niall Wilson, the *O.C.L.T.* occult thriller series. His tie-in work contains novels for *Star Trek*, *Warhammer*, *WarCraft*, and *Eureka*. He has written children's books, including the original series Pete and Penny's Pizza Puzzles, the award-winning *Bandslam: The Junior Novel*, and the #1 best-selling *42: The Jackie Robinson Story*. Aaron has also written educational books on a variety of topics and over seventy roleplaying games, such as the original games *Asylum*, *Spookshow*, and *Chosen*, work for White Wolf, Wizards of the Coast, Fantasy Flight, Pinnacle, and many others, and both the Origins Award-winning *Gamemastering Secrets* and the Gold ENnie-winning *Lure of the Lich Lord*. He is the co-creator of the *ReDeus* series, and one of the founders of Crazy 8 Press. Aaron lives in New York with his family. You can follow him online at gryphonrose.com, on Facebook at facebook.com/gryphonrose, and on Twitter @gryphonrose.

Curious about other Crossroad Press books?
Stop by our site:
http://store.crossroadpress.com
We offer quality writing
in digital, audio, and print formats.

Enter the code FIRSTBOOK
to get 20% off your first order from our store!
Stop by today!

www.ingramcontent.com/pod-product-compliance
Lightning Source LLC
Chambersburg PA
CBHW060427180626
46817CB00007B/2696